Enough small talk

"Talking with you never got me anywhere, Katy. I am going to do what I should have done years ago—take you to bed and make love to you until you are so damned senseless that you will agree to anything."

She forced herself to ignore the pressure of his fingers on her jaw, and, raising her eyes to his, she arched one perfectly shaped brow derisively. "Honestly, Jake, darling, I had no idea you could be so dramatic." She forced a laugh. "But the evening is over now, and I think you'd better leave."

"Oh, no, Katy, darling," he said, mimicking her words. His hand closed on the lapel of her robe. "It is only one-thirty and I have paid until two."

D1167571

JACQUELINE BAIRD hails from Northeast England. She is married and has two sons. She especially enjoys traveling, and has many more ideas stored away for future novels.

JACQUELINE BAIRD

Dishonourable Proposal

Harlequin Books

TORONTO • NEW YORK • LONDON
AMSTERDAM • PARIS • SYDNEY • HAMBURG
STOCKHOLM • ATHENS • TOKYO • MILAN
MADRID • WARSAW • BUDAPEST • AUCKLAND

Harlequin Presents first edition May 1993
ISBN 0-373-11558-X

Original hardcover edition published in 1992
by Mills & Boon Limited

DISHONOURABLE PROPOSAL

CHAPTER ONE

LENA shot a final look at her reflection in the mirror placed strategically behind the side-curtain of the stage. What she saw caused a wry smile to curve her full lips. A tall, beautiful girl with luminous green eyes, a short straight nose and a soft full-lipped mouth. Long blonde hair skilfully arranged in ringlets peeked beneath the exquisite lace of a bridal veil. She looked like a Gainsborough lady, the dress a magnificent confection in satin and lace. The finale and Claude's *pièce de résistance* of the charity fashion show.

A shadow darkened her lustrous eyes; once, years ago, she had dreamed of wearing just such a gown for a very special man, but not any more...

Straightening her shoulders and plastering a smile on her face, she stepped out on to the stage, and glided down the catwalk. Keeping her head high, her glance skimmed the illustrious audience. The baronial hall appeared to be full. Fluidly she moved, pausing, turning, her smile for everyone and no one, then finally one last turn and she was retreating through the curtain and off stage to tumultuous applause.

Lena smiled for the small group of photographers outside the hotel, and with a few lithe strides sank gratefully into the back seat of the gleaming white Rolls-Royce waiting at the kerb.

It was a beautiful August evening; even London sparkled in the red of the setting sun, the buildings tinged with pink and gold. She straightened the close-fitting black dress over her thighs, and sighed. One more performance for the benefit of an elderly couple, then—a small smile tugged at her full lips—Lena Lawrence would be no more. Kathleen Lawrence Meldenton would resurface, hopefully as a designer and possibly as a businesswoman.

'We have arrived, madam.'

The polite words of the chauffeur brought her out of her reverie, and, looking out of the window, she noted they had stopped outside a large elegant apartment building overlooking the Thames. The chauffeur opened the door, but before she could say thank you the breath stuck in her throat as another voice, deep and melodious, echoed her thought, and the large figure of a man slid into the back seat beside her.

'Hello, Katy. It has been a long time, and you're as beautiful as ever, though I'm not sure I like all this make-up,' and with a casual intimate gesture one long tanned finger tilted up her chin. 'Your mouth's hanging open. Is that an invitation to a kiss, Katy, darling?' the deep voice drawled, while glittering black eyes stared down at her with open amusement. 'Or should I call you Lena?'

No one except her father had called her Katy in years, though she intended changing that after tonight. Her heartbeat thundered in her breast as she looked up into the darkly handsome face of the large man crowding her into the corner of the back seat of the Rolls.

Jake Granton... What evil trick of fate had brought him to this street at this precise moment, she did not know, but shock and a fast-rising anger made her creamy complexion flush furiously.

'Just what the hell do you think you're doing? Get out of this car immediately,' she snapped angrily.

Then she was blushing for a totally different reason as dark eyes slid blatantly over her face, the gold hair tumbling around her shoulders, down to the soft swell of her full breasts, partially exposed by the sexy little black knitted cotton sheath dress. Jake Granton's eyes lingered appreciatively on her breasts then slid lower to her thighs and the elegant curve of her long legs.

The dress started under her armpits and ended above her knees. It was one of Claude's, designed for the youthful end of the fashion market, and she wished like hell she had not let Claude talk her into wearing it tonight.

She wanted to pull her skirt down, fold her arms over her chest. Her Lena Lawrence image was not for this man, and his obvious sexual appraisal made her skin prickle with totally unwanted awareness.

'Are you deaf or something? I said get out!' she cried, desperately clinging to her anger. In her peripheral vision she saw the chauffeur, an uncertain look on his lined face, his hand hesitant on the door, unsure whether to close it.

'Is everything all right, madam?' he enquired politely.

'No.'

'Yes,' the deep voice drowned her out. 'I am the lady's date for this evening, and I paid three thousand pounds for the privilege. Check the card the agency gave you. Jake Granton, the penthouse, Albermarle Towers.'

Lena watched in stunned amazement as the chauffeur withdrew a card from his pocket, read it, then checked the card with the wallet Jake flashed at him.

'That appears to be correct, sir,' and with a brief glance at Lena he closed the car door and, walking to the front of the car, slid into the driving seat and started the engine.

'Now just a minute,' she spluttered ineffectually as the car moved off into the London traffic.

'Lena, I am surprised. Your sophisticated image is slipping badly. That is hardly fair to me, a devoted member of your drooling public,' he drawled with mocking amusement.

With a terrific effort of self-control, Lena forced herself to think clearly. There must be a mistake somewhere, but she had a sinking feeling it was she who had made it.

'I don't know what you're playing at, Jake, but I had a date with a kindly old grey-haired gentleman and his wife; perhaps you would care to explain,' she said coolly.

'The grey-haired gentleman was my agent at the auction, and he did say it was for someone else. If you check with your friend Claude, you will find I am right.'

She did not need to check, as she thought back over the night in question. Two days ago she had arrived in London from France to appear as the star model in a glittering charity fashion show given by Claude, the top Paris designer, in aid of leukaemia research.

It had been held in the stately home of a belted earl, and the tickets alone had cost the guests a fantastic amount of money. The proceedings had culminated in an auction, the prizes varying from a cruise in a luxury yacht to the tie of a member of the royal family. Lena had allowed herself to be talked into offering herself as a dinner companion for the evening, and had been amazed at the money a simple date with a top fashion model had engendered. Her fame, such as it was, she had acquired more by accident than design.

As a nineteen-year-old living in Paris at her friend Anna's home and attending art college, she had met Claude, the father of Anna's boyfriend Alain. When Claude had suggested she model for him she had laughed. She was the right height at five-nine, but she was also full-breasted. Claude had dismissed her objections with a wave of his hand. Apparently the stick-like figures of bygone years were no longer fashionable and it was perfectly all right for a model to have a bust these days.

The idea of earning some money of her own, instead of being completely dependent on her father until she left college, appealed to her. To Lena's amazement, by the time she had completed her college course her face had appeared on the cover of *Vogue*.

When Claude had branched out from *haute couture* into lingerie, it was Lena's face and figure that had appeared in all the magazines and hoardings, clad in a white basque, briefs, garter belt, and stockings. That had been her one mistake in an otherwise very enjoyable career. She had never dreamed the picture would have such impact, and before she knew it she was voted the official pin-up for the French navy, and was described as the sexiest thing on two legs.

She still modelled high fashion and in the past year she had graced the cover of *Vogue* several times, but to her chagrin the celebrity status she had achieved worldwide was mostly due to that one pin-up picture, and she bitterly regretted ever allowing Claude to talk her into it. Now she was newsworthy and she did not much like it.

She had expected the charity gala to be her last public appearance; at twenty-two, she was ready to get back to her first love—design. No one except Claude was aware of the fact, and she could not blame him for milking her last appearance for all it was worth as the charity concerned was very dear to his heart. But it did not stop her feeling angry towards him. She knew she was being unfair. But it was Claude's fault she had ended up in this car with the last man in the world she wanted to be with.

She squirmed uncomfortably on the plush leather seat, casting a furious glance at her silent companion, and she longed to knock the smug grin off his handsome face.

Lena had taken part in the auction because of Anna, the daughter of a French diplomat; she had been Lena's friend from her first day at boarding-school. She had nicknamed the lanky Kathleen 'Lena', and had been there for Katy when her naïve dream of marriage and happily ever after had collapsed round her head at the tender age of eighteen. Later it had been Anna's suggestion she use the name Lena in her modelling career.

It still seemed too incredible to believe that the petite dark-haired laughing girl was no more. Lena had been bridesmaid at her wedding, and godmother to her daughter. But a short twelve months previous Anna had gone in to hospital for a few simple tests for anaemia, and within four months was dead. A shadow of sorrow darkened Lena's expressive green eyes as for a moment she was lost in the past. With a start she heard her name called.

'Lena Lawrence, darling of the masses, sophisticated lady, struck dumb. You disappoint me, Lena.'

She turned a blistering glance on the man beside her. 'I have nothing to say to you, except get lost!'

'Tut, tut, whatever happened to sweet little biddable Katy?'

She took a deep breath, reminding herself she was a sophisticated successful woman, not a mutely adoring teenager. 'She grew up,' she said coldly.

When she had been persuaded to offer herself on a dinner date for charity, never in her wildest dreams or worst nightmares had she envisaged ending up with Jake Granton... He had hurt her terribly once, and she had never forgiven him, or forgotten...Unfortunately he still had the power to hurt her; his masculine aura was like a force field sucking her in. She recognised that she was aware of the man with every fibre of her being, and deplored the fact.

She remembered her relief when the bidding had finally stopped at an incredible three thousand pounds, offered by an elderly gentleman near the back of the room. She had congratulated him personally and been doubly relieved when she had heard as she'd walked away the old man mention that another person was coming. The date had been for either one or two people and Lena had much preferred the idea of dining out with a couple. The man had said it was for someone else, and she, in her hurry to leave, had obviously misheard him.

'Well, isn't this nice? Quite like old times,' and Lena nearly jumped out of the seat as a strong brown hand curved over her knee.

With an angry shove she removed his hand from her knee. 'Hardly,' she snapped. 'I don't remember you ever taking me out for the evening, and certainly not to dinner in a white Rolls.' Her caustic reply was a brave attempt to mask her furiously beating heart. Her knee still tingled where he had touched her, and she was disgusted with her own reaction.

'No, I didn't; an oversight on my part,' he said reflectively. 'But if I had would it have made you accept my proposal, Lena?' He did not wait for her answer. 'I think not. You are a very sensual woman and, if half the rumours about you are true, you like variety. I was a fool to imagine you would commit yourself to one man, but not any more. So tonight we will enjoy each other, hmm? No strings attached.'

'No.' She turned slightly in her seat to face him, no trace of the turmoil he had caused visible in her cool expression.

Jake Granton was supposedly a friend of her father's, and also a shareholder in Meldenton China, her family's company. She had considered the possibility that she might have to face Jake Granton again once she took up employment in the family firm, but she had convinced herself the likelihood was remote. Jake's father had died a couple of years ago and Jake had inherited Granton Holdings. The dividend from his Meldenton China shares were a mere drop in the ocean to a man of his wealth.

She considered herself mature enough to treat him with cool civility. Unfortunately, meeting him unexpectedly and as Lena Lawrence, model, she felt at a terrible disadvantage.

'I don't know why you did this, Jake,' she continued, and with gathering confidence she added, 'but there is absolutely no point in our spending the evening together. I'll tell the chauffeur to turn around and take you home, and don't worry, I will refund your three thousand pounds.'

She was proud of her steady voice as she casually dismissed the evening as a mistake, but inside she was quaking in case he didn't accept her offer. The date was supposed to be from eight until two, dinner and dancing, and there was no way she wanted to spend that long in this man's company. She did not dare...

She studied him surreptitiously beneath her thick lashes. It was two years since the last time they had met and that had ended in a furious row. She did some quick mental arithmetic: he must be thirty-four now, but from what she could see of him he had not developed an ounce of fat on his tall muscular frame.

His straight black hair, worn slightly longer than was the present fashion, was parted at the side and swept casually back off his broad forehead. His perfectly arched brows shaded deep-set dark brown, almost black eyes, fringed with thick curling lashes, a legacy from his Italian mother. His nose was straight, but at the moment, she realised, his nostrils were flaring dangerously wide over a sensuous mouth that was tight with anger.

'No. I was stupid enough to allow you to dismiss me twice in the past, but not this time.'

Her eyes widened at the icy anger in his tone. His dark gaze caught and held hers, and she was powerless to break the contact.

'You, L-e-n-a L-a-w-r-e-n-c-e,' he drawled her professional name as if it were a dirty word, 'are going to entertain me for the next few hours. I have paid dearly for the privilege.' His full lips curved in a cynical grin. 'Tell me, is five hundred an hour the going rate nowadays?'

Rage surged through her body at his implication, and, lifting her hand, she struck out at his handsome mocking face. But before the blow connected he caught her slender wrist in a grip of steel.

'Now, now, Lena, temper, temper. Surely you don't want to arrive at the restaurant with your partner's face bearing your fingermarks? No doubt the efficient Claude has arranged for the Press to be on hand—think what the publicity would do to your model-girl image.'

'You're hurting my wrist,' she bit out between clenched teeth. Determinedly she counted silently to a hundred to prevent herself screaming at him like a banshee. His hold gentled on her wrist, but if anything it was worse, as Jake's thumb gently stroked her inner wrist, sending an electric current of awareness shooting up her arm. Then to her utter amazement his dark eyes softened on her flushed and furious face.

'I apologise, Lena; my less than flattering comments were uncalled for.'

She shivered, although the evening was warm. She had told herself she was over Jake years ago, but as they sat in the close confines of the luxury car the subtle male scent of him teased her nostrils, which, she despairingly admitted to herself, she would recognise if she were deaf, dumb and blind as uniquely Jake.

'I wouldn't hurt you for the world.' And for a fleeting instant she saw something she did not recognise in his eyes before he partially lowered his lashes, masking his expression. But she quickly dismissed the notion as he added hardily, 'But I will have you tonight, Lena, darling.'

She took a deep breath and forced herself to ignore his last statement; perhaps if she tried to keep it light, or reason with him... 'Jake, I've known you since I was fourteen. Why bother bidding at a charity auction for a date? You could have just called me.'

'And of course you would have said yes,' he mocked, his dark eyes gleaming with devilment. 'Does that mean I could have had a freebie...? Damn,' he chuckled, 'I should have realised; they do say a woman never forgets her first lover.'

'Why, you arrogant, conceited pig...' All thoughts of reasoning with the man flew from her mind as she almost choked with rage. 'How——?' How dared he remind her of the one night they had spent together?

He cut her off before she could complete the sentence. 'Shh, Lena, we've arrived; prepare to face the Press.'

Flushed and shaking with anger, she watched as Jake unfurled his long frame and slid out of the door the chauffeur was holding open. Behind him she saw a smattering of photographers, and it was only with the greatest effort of self-control that she was able to slide along the seat and accept the hand Jake held out to her.

She flashed a mutinous look at his darkly handsome face and saw a grimace of disgust twist his sensuous mouth as one photographer, more pushy than most, knelt on the pavement and took what she knew could only be a rather revealing picture as she bent to get out of the car, all long legs and revealing much more cleavage than was normal.

She pasted a smile on her face and linked her arm through Jake's, leaning slightly against him. She felt him tense, and felt a fleeting sense of triumph: he was not immune to her, after all. As for the publicity, he would hate it. His staid banker image would take a knock tonight. Serves him right, she thought gleefully.

Photographers she could handle, and did. She smoothed one slender hand over her hip, highlighting the beautiful appliqué butterfly in red and gold that curved across the midriff of the skimpy dress, lifting the style from the mundane to the exotic. She owed it to Claude to show off his design to the best advantage, and the fact that it was one of her own drawings he had adopted for the motif gave her an added sense of pride. With another brilliant smile for the Press, she allowed Jake to lead her into the exclusive French restaurant in the heart of Mayfair.

At first glance the restaurant appeared to be full, but within seconds of entering the place the head waiter was at Lena's side. His dark eyes flashed appreciatively over her as he bowed courteously, declaring it was a great pleasure to see her in his restaurant and leading them swiftly to a small table for two set in the very centre of the room.

Beside her, Jake, every inch the dominant male, immaculately dressed in a dark dinner suit and snowy-white shirt, exuded an elusive aura that went with wealth and sophistication. As every man's head in the place turned to watch Lena sit at the table, so too did every woman's head turn to study her strikingly attractive companion.

Why wouldn't they? Lena thought wryly. She had almost forgotten how overwhelmingly masculine he was and it helped that he was a millionaire many times over.

Thankfully she accepted the menu from the waiter, and assumed her role as hostess with a sophistication she was proud of. She would show Jake she was no young girl to be intimidated by his potent brand of charm.

'What would you like to eat, Jake? I'm going to have avocado and salmon mousse, followed by the monkfish with the mild curry sauce, plus the fresh vegetables. How about you? The same?'

She arched one perfectly shaped brow enquiringly at the man seated opposite her as she placed the menu on the table. She was still in shock, but she had controlled her earlier anger and was determined to take charge.

He met her cool look with an equally chilling smile before turning to the hovering waiter and rattling off her order and a main dish of peppered steak in cream sauce for himself, plus a bottle of vintage champagne.

'I may be your guest, Lena, but I never allow a woman to order for me, or to me...' His dark eyes flashed with a hint of anger then softened perceptibly as his gaze roamed blatantly down to the soft curve of her full breasts.

She felt a flush of heat creep from her stomach to cover her whole body at his sensuous explicit look, and bitterly she cursed Claude under her breath. If only she had known who it was she was dining with she would have conveniently developed a dreaded lurgy of some kind. Jake had the capacity to make her feel like a gauche teenager with just one glance from his knowing brown eyes.

'Except, perhaps, in bed, and then I don't mind if the lady takes the initiative. Sometimes it can be quite exciting...' He laughed out loud at her shocked expression. 'Don't you agree?' he teased.

'Do you think you could possibly bring your mind out of the gutter long enough for us to enjoy our meal with some semblance of civility?' she said curtly. She was sick to death of his crude innuendoes.

'A truce, Lena, hmm?'

'And there's no need for you to call me Lena. You always called me Katy when we were f—friends.' She hesitated on the word 'friends', then blundered on. 'It is only in France I'm known as Lena. Now I'm home I prefer Katy.'

'Friend. I once had a friend called Katy, but I don't see her in the woman before me now. Would you like to know what I do see?'

'Not particularly, but I have no doubt you will tell me anyway,' she said with a small laugh to cover the swift unexpected stab of hurt she felt at his denial of their friendship. It was stupid, she knew; they had not been close in four years, but before that she had believed he was her friend and more...

'I see a very beautiful, very sexy young woman who has spent the last few years playing on those attributes, with great success. How does it feel, Lena—sorry, Katy— to know most of the men in two continents go to bed fantasising about your body? Does it turn you on?'

'I'm a model,' she said flatly, and watched in amazement as Jake flung his head back and burst out laughing. 'I don't see what is so funny in that.'

'Oh, come on...I saw the poster of you—it was on hoardings all over the world.' He was still chuckling as his brown eyes caught and held hers. 'Claude must have made millions on that line. The original Eve could not

have done better. Every man who saw it spent hours
wondering how that basque stayed over your nipples and
waiting for it to slip.'

Her lips parted in an answering grin; she could not
help herself. Her basic honesty forced her to admit that
his opinion of the photograph was spot-on. She had been
really quite well-covered, wearing a lot more than most
women wore on a beach, but the photographer had shot
her reaching for an apple on a tree.

'They would have had a long wait,' she giggled. 'I had
it stuck to my flesh with strong tape.'

'Ah, another illusion bites the dust.' Jake groaned
theatrically, and for the first time that evening they
shared a smile of mutual amusement.

The waiter arrived with the food and for the rest of
the meal Jake encouraged Katy to talk about her modelling career. By carefully avoiding anything personal and
sticking strictly to the kind of chat she would give to
any interviewer, they managed to get to the coffee stage
without an angry word.

Katy quite happily spooned sugar into her cup and
followed it with a hefty dollop of cream. The evening
had not been half as bad as she'd first feared on seeing
Jake was to be her companion. She could only hope the
rest of the evening, at the nightclub, went as well . . . She
stopped in the process of lifting the cup to her mouth.
What was she thinking of? Enjoying Jake's company?
She took a swift gulp of coffee and replaced her cup on
the table.

He had been charming and courteous, and had fooled
her yet again . . . Which, she thought cynically, considering he believed she was little better than a whore,
and had said as much, tonight and two years ago, only
underlined what she had first discovered as a shy
eighteen-year-old, fathoms deep in love with the man.

He was a devious, ruthless devil, who could quite happily
stab one in the back while smiling into one's face.

'Don't you have to watch your figure in your
business?' Jake queried, glancing at her creamy coffee,
then more leisurely at her bare shoulders and firm
breasts. A lazy smile curved his sensuous lips as his dark
eyes finally made contact with Katy's.

She easily recognised the male appreciation and the
hint of more on offer in his dark gaze. How many
women, she wondered, had fallen for that seductive smile
and the potent masculine virility of the man over the
years? Hundreds, no doubt. Her own stepmother Monica
among them, she thought bitterly. Yet no hint of scandal
ever touched him; to the world at large he was a highly
respectable but rather boring banker.

Carefully she raised her cup to her mouth and took
another sip of coffee to give herself time to control the
swift stab of angry self-disgust she felt that she had once
been stupid enough to be one of his women.

Replacing her cup on the saucer, she finally answered
his question. 'Why should I?' She fluttered her ridicu-
lously long lashes. 'There are thousands of men to do
it for me, darling.' She laughed, playing the flirt for all
she was worth.

'Of course, how could I forget the pin-up of the
decade?' he drawled sarcastically, his earlier easy charm
vanishing as with a bitter look at her beautiful face he
beckoned the waiter for the bill.

Chalk up one for me, she thought confidently, though
why Jake should feel bitter Katy couldn't imagine; that
was her prerogative, surely? Still, she was finally proving
mature enough to handle him; perhaps the rest of the
evening would not be such a trial after all. Reaching out
her hand, she said, 'You're my guest; I'll take care of

that,' as the waiter placed the plate with the folded paper beside Jake.

'No, you won't,' he almost snarled and, throwing a bundle of notes on the table, he glanced at the fine gold Rolex circling his wrist and stood up. 'Come along. It's almost eleven; the car will be waiting. Let's get the rest of this farce over with.'

She could not understand why his former easy charm had suddenly changed to bitter anger, but he was not ordering her about. 'Farce!' she snapped. 'May I remind you it was all your idea? You didn't have to bid; you're rich enough—you could have just given the money to the charity.'

She was talking to his back as he headed for the door of the restaurant, but his innate good manners forced him to wait at the entrance for her. She deliberately made for the powder-room, and dawdled over combing her hair and repairing her lipstick.

By the time they were once more seated in the back seat of the Rolls Jake's face was flushed dark with rage at the delay. Katy had to hide a smile behind a cough. Serves him right, she thought gleefully. He strode through life as if he were God's gift to women; it would do him no harm to wait for one for a change.

'I'm glad you found that amusing, but I don't appreciate being kept waiting,' he grated.

'Sorry,' she drawled, but she could not keep the amusement from her voice.

'You will be if you keep me waiting again tonight,' he said stonily.

Katy made no comment. It's better to quit when you're ahead, she told herself, and settled back into the plush leather upholstery. She imagined she could feel the heat of his thigh burning into hers, but her common sense told her they were not even touching.

She chanced a glance at his face. His hooded lids closed half over his eyes, masking his expression; his mouth was set in a tight line. His ruggedly attractive face had a curious brooding quality about it. Totally different from the laughing young man she had once known. This cold remote man was a stranger to her, and that was how she wanted it to stay...

'I asked you if you want more champagne, and I would appreciate it if you would acknowledge me when I speak to you.'

They had barely spoken since leaving the restaurant and now, as they sat at a comfortable table in Annabel's, Katy's head shot up with a jerk at the sound of Jake's obviously angry voice. Lost in her own thoughts, she had not been aware he had spoken.

'Yes, please,' she responded coolly.

The champagne arrived and she watched as the waiter carefully filled the long fluted glass, and her eyes widened as a squat tumbler of what looked like whisky and soda was placed in front of Jake.

'Aren't you sharing the champagne? It is a waste of the bottle—I'll never drink all that.'

'I need something stronger,' he replied tautly, and, lifting his glass, he took a long swallow of the fiery liquid, put the glass back on the table, and raised his head, his brown eyes oddly enigmatic as they clashed with hers. 'Though I might share one with you later.'

She did not trust his sensuous smile. He needed something stronger; perhaps he had the right idea—getting drunk would be one way of getting through the next few hours, Katy thought wryly. In the dim intimate atmosphere of the nightclub, the shock of seeing Jake again was beginning to wear off, and some of his earlier comments had begun to sound vaguely threatening as they registered in her stunned mind.

'Have you seen David, your father, recently?'

'What? Oh, no, about eighteen months ago,' Katy replied, flustered by his steady gaze and the incongruity of the question. She had been busily thinking of his earlier statement that he would have her tonight. She had thought it was the kind of sophisticated teasing she had encountered dozens of times before in the modelling world, where every man seemed to consider fashion models easy game... But now, with his changed attitude, she was not so sure, and yes, she was panicking...

'You do know Monica and David are divorced, or does your family interest you so little now you are a *celebrity*?' The last comment was a sneer.

Katy sat up straighter in her chair, the mention of Monica enough to stiffen her spine. 'Yes. I may not see Father very often, but there is such a thing as a telephone,' she informed him sarcastically. 'Not that my communications with my father are any of your business.'

CHAPTER TWO

ON SUNDAY Katy was lunching with her father; they had never been particularly close—she had always considered him a womaniser—but as the years had passed she had come to accept he was no worse than most men.

Tomorrow she was going to tell him she was joining the family business, Meldenton China, makers of fine china. A frown marred her smooth brow as she recalled her conversation the previous day with Mr Jeffries, the family solicitor, and the other trustee, along with her father, of the inheritance her grandmother had left her—a thirty per cent share in the family firm.

She had a troubled feeling there was something the elderly man was not telling her. She gave a dismissive shrug of her elegant shoulders. She was twenty-two now, and the trusteeship was at an end. She had planned for this day for a long time...

Circumstances had led her into a different career from the one she had intended. There was no point in denying she had enjoyed her success as a model, and now it was over she felt a tinge of sadness. She had made some good friends in the fashion business, and she had travelled all over the world, but she knew deep down that she had always been acting a part. It had been a game she'd played, albeit very successfully.

She conceded it had taught her a lot. Claude had encouraged her to keep up her interest in design and on numerous occasions used some of her work for ornamentation. She had enjoyed the experience, but now she was happily anticipating a new job as a designer of fine

23

china with the family firm—the career she had originally trained for at art college.

Katy jumped and spilled a little of the champagne as
Jake reached across the table and caught her free hand.
Lost in thought, she had almost forgotten his stinging
comment accusing her of ignoring her father.

'It was not my intention to argue with you tonight,
Katy,' brown eyes clashed and mingled with green, 'but
your father is an old friend.'

The use of her given name lent sincerity to his words.
Obviously he had taken her early remonstration to heart,
and the thought pleased her...until she heard 'old friend'.
Oh, no! She wasn't falling for his easy charm, his lies...

'Then mind your own business,' she snapped back,
pulling her hand away. With a friend like Jake, who
needed enemies? she thought venomously.

'As a friend of the family I think I am entitled to
interfere. Your father is getting old, you have barely seen
him in four years, and now he is on his own he's bound
to be lonely. If you weren't so wrapped up in your career,
so damn selfish, you might have noticed.' Jake's scathing
tone made her hackles rise. He had a damn nerve, she
thought furiously as she listened to him berating her.

'My God! Your father's house is not ten minutes away
from the hotel you are staying in. Hardly the caring
daughter, are you?'

'Such regard for my father I find rather hypocritical,
coming from you,' Katy shot back angrily. How dared
he pretend concern for the man, when she knew to her
cost Jake had been Monica's lover long before her father
had married the woman, and probably still was? For her
London home one could read *ménage à trois*—her father,
Monica and Jake. Katy herself had had a lucky escape
from the machinations of Jake once before and there

was no way she was going to sit here and listen to his
hypocritical cant.

'Just what do you mean by that?' Jake demanded,
and as she would have risen from the table his large hand
caught her wrist and forced her to sit down.

She pulled her wrist free, but only because he allowed
her to, and quite deliberately she refilled her glass and,
raising it to her lips, drained the sparkling liquid. How
dared he question her, the swine? And without thinking
she refilled her glass again.

'I asked you a question. I have been called many names
in my time, but never a hypocrite; what exactly are you
implying?' he demanded hardily.

'Nothing,' she muttered, and, picking up her glass,
she drained the sparkling contents thirstily. She did not
like to remember that particular painful episode in her
life. 'You need not worry about my father. I'm going to
see him tomorrow.'

'You've been in London days already. How gracious
of you, sparing an hour or two for him before jetting
off again with your French friend. But then, beneath the
sophisticated image you are still a spoilt, selfish little
girl,' Jake intoned furiously. 'I had hoped you might
have changed...'

Katy carefully refilled her glass, and drained it yet
again. Her hand shook with the force of the rage boiling
inside her. She *had* changed; she was no more the dumb
girl he could manipulate. His sneering superiority was
the last straw. For years she had avoided having a show-
down with this man, preferring to hide her hurt under
various excuses, but not any more; she was going to tell
him just what a rat fink... No. Katy took a deep calming
breath: she was a sophisticated lady; she would not give
him the satisfaction of losing her temper. Instead she
answered coolly, 'I am not jetting off anywhere. I am

going to my father's house tomorrow and I expect to stay. I am joining the family firm—something I have always wanted to do.'

'You, Lena Lawrence, working nine to five, pushing paper? Don't make me laugh,' he mocked cynically, but his dark eyes were fixed with a strange intensity upon her beautiful flushed face.

His mockery broke the slender thread of her self-control. 'No, not Lena Lawrence, but Katy Lawrence Meldenton. You were instrumental in stopping me once before, but not this time, buster. I know you for the rat you are. "Hypocrite" doesn't begin to describe you.'

'I think you'd better explain that remark. I always treated you with the utmost care and consideration; I offered you my name, everything. Nothing would have pleased me more than having you stay in London. I did not chase you away, you ran... You wanted to see the world,' he said harshly, his mouth twisting cynically. 'Or so you said.'

She had told him that, and now she had almost admitted she had lied. She reached for her glass; she needed to regain her self-control before she gave away more than she wanted him to know.

'Why do you dislike me so much? Do I prick your conscience?' Jake continued seriously. His long fingers curved around her hand on the stem of the glass. 'No more drink,' he warned hardily.

She looked down at his tanned fingers, then up into his black eyes; he was leaning over the table towards her, his face expressionless; only the glitter in the depths of his dark eyes betrayed his tightly controlled anger. 'I've put up with a lot from you over the years, Katy, because I valued our,' he hesitated, 'relationship, for want of a better word, but no one talks to me the way you have tonight and gets away with it. I want the truth and now.'

What truth? Katy thought. If she told him she knew of his infidelity all those years ago, with her own step-mother, what would it prove? Only how deeply he had hurt her. He was an astute man. He would realise just how much she had loved him . . . No, it was much better to let him think she had had a change of heart. Her young emotions were fickle. She would rather have him believe she was a flighty, promiscuous lady than let him know how vulnerable she really was. Pride was all she'd had left her when she'd walked out on him at eighteen. It would be foolish to surrender it now in the heat of anger.

'I'm waiting, Katy.'

So much anger and hurt—too many emotions were surfacing tonight, and she wanted nothing more than to get back to the hotel as quickly as possible, before she said something she would regret.

'Can we leave now? I've had enough. I'll refund you the money if it's not two yet.' She stood up and swayed slightly—her legs felt none too steady—but in seconds Jake was beside her, his arm going around her waist to support her. He bent his dark head towards her blonde one.

'I will take you back to the hotel, but first answer me.'

Half drunk she might be, but she still recognised Jake's determination. 'Does it matter?' she said wearily; raking over the past was a futile exercise.

'Yes, I think it matters a great deal to me,' Jake responded. He turned her to face him, his arms crossed around her waist, holding her close against his hard body. 'Tell me. Why do you say I was responsible for preventing you from working at Meldenton years ago? Why do you think I am a hypocrite?' he questioned adamantly. 'Make me understand.'

She raised her head and looked up into the dark piercing eyes burning down into hers. She felt the heat of his body, the hard length of his muscular thighs pressed against her slender limbs. The tension in him communicated to her even though her head was swimming. She had to get out into the fresh air, away from Jake, but first she had to answer him.

'You seduced me when I was eighteen, the daughter of your "good friend", and now have the gall to condemn my lifestyle.'

'Seduced!' he exclaimed. 'You were begging for it.'

She ignored his exclamation, and his crude comment. 'Oh, come on, Jake,' she drawled, forcing her lips into what she hoped was a confident smile while her mind searched frantically for something to say without admitting she knew about Monica. Slowly her smile turned into a rueful grimace. 'Remember when we had sex . . .' she could not say 'made love' ' . . . I asked you if I was the first woman you had loved, and you told me I was the first and only woman you had loved? God, but I was naïve—I actually believed you were a virgin as well. Instead I was only one in a long line.' She noted with interest the dull flush that burnt up under his skin. 'What would you call it, Jake—the old double standard or hypocrisy? I know what I'd call it.' Katy snorted, and before he could respond she added, 'By the way, when did you last visit Dad, your "good friend"?' she asked spitefully.

Jake's hands fell to his sides and she was free. She shot a quick glance at his face and to her surprise she saw guilt registered there . . .

'It must be nearly a year; I have been out of the country a lot,' he qualified, avoiding her eyes.

By sheer luck she had hit a nerve. Of course he wouldn't have visited her father, she thought bitterly.

Once Monica had left, her father's house would have held no appeal for him.

'Rather the pot calling the kettle black, Jake,' she derided.

Katy did not see the angry bitterness in his eyes when he lifted his head and looked around the room as if he had just realised where they were. He turned back to her and for an instant the tension was electric. She thought he wanted to shake her, but instead Jake straightened his broad shoulders, and clasped her elbow in his strong hand.

'This is no place to explain, to talk,' he said flatly. 'We're leaving.'

Her legs almost buckled when the fresh air hit her, and if it had not been for Jake's hand supporting her she would have crumbled to the ground at his feet. Living mostly in France for the past few years, she was quite used to drinking wine, but in the club she had drunk four glasses in quick succession.

A camera flash went off in her face. She closed her eyes and instinctively turned, hiding her face in the warmth of Jake's broad chest. She groaned inwardly: the Press would have a field-day. It was the last coherent thought she had for some time.

'Are you all right? Can you walk, or shall I carry you to your room?'

Katy opened her eyes. Jake was leaning over her, his darkly handsome face frowning his concern, or more likely disgust, she thought ruefully. She had rather gone over the top in the past couple of hours. She was still feeling woozy, but at least she could recognise they were in the Rolls, parked outside the Inn on the Park, her hotel.

From her alcohol-hazed mind she managed to gather enough self-control to reply slowly, 'Thank you. I can walk perfectly well.' She crossed her fingers in hope. 'There is no need for you to accompany me.' And with what little elegance she could muster she slid out of the car, to stand, swaying slightly, on the pavement. She took one step before a large arm circled her waist and almost dragged her up the steps to the hotel entrance.

'You little fool, for all your sophisticated airs, you shouldn't be allowed out alone,' Jake said bluntly, before turning to the reception desk and demanding her key.

Katy could not fail to notice the expression of knowing male complicity on the young man's face as he handed Jake her key, and she stepped back out of Jake's reach.

'Do you want coffee sent up?' he demanded.

'No, thank you. I never drink coffee at night,' she confessed. The young receptionist's look had sobered her up quicker than coffee ever would.

'May I have my key, please?' She held out her hand to Jake. There was no way he was coming upstairs with her. She was not that intoxicated.

Instead of giving her the key Jake caught her outstretched hand in his, 'I always see my dates safely to their doors, Katy.' His wide mouth twitched with a hint of suppressed humour, and, tightening his grip on her hand, he urged her towards the bank of lifts. 'And you would not want to spoil that young man's pleasure. He will be fantasising about you and me all night.'

'Not all night, Jake.' She glanced at the slim gold watch on her wrist. 'Another forty minutes and your time is up, and it can't be a moment too soon for me,' she avowed bluntly, leaving him in no doubt that she considered the evening a duty not a date.

'In that case I'd better not waste any more time,' he said silkily, and as the lift door closed behind them he turned her into his arms.

His mouth moved forcibly against hers, evoking a multitude of memories she would rather have suppressed. His hands slid down her back to press her hard against his taut frame. His teeth bit into her lower lip, demanding that she give him access, abandon herself to the passionate awareness that had simmered beneath the surface between them all night.

Fury at his presumption battled with a rising tide of excitement she could barely control. She wanted to give in to his erotic demand, lose herself in the heady pleasure of his kiss, but she did not dare; he must never know how easily he could reduce her to a state of mindless, aching desire.

She raised her foot and stepped down hard on his, her stiletto heel sinking into the soft leather of his shoe. He dropped her like a hot potato, and hopped around the lift, holding his foot.

'What the hell did you do that for? You've almost lamed me!' Jake thundered, his eyes hardening to chips of jet.

The lift door slid open, and Katy shot out. She didn't like the glint in Jake's eye—it promised retaliation—but she could not repress a chuckle; he had looked funny hopping around on one leg.

'Don't play me for a fool, Katy, or you'll live to regret it,' he threatened, before adding pointedly, 'If you thought you had seen the worst of my temper in Paris that was nothing to what I could do now.'

She already bitterly regretted ever having met him, and she flinched at his reminder of Paris. He had turned her life upside-down once, and had tried a second time, but no way was he doing it a third time. 'Open the door, please,' she muttered, not looking at him. If she could just nip inside and slam it in his face... She watched his tanned hand insert the key in the lock, but in an ungentlemanly move for Jake he walked into the room first.

'Thank you,' she murmured politely, and, brushing past him, she made a beeline for the bedroom and the safety of the bathroom.

'Katy! Damn you, I'm not finished with you yet, not by a long way.'

'So write me a letter,' she replied cheekily.

She made it and locked the door behind her, Jake's cry of outrage ringing in her ears. A cold shower—that's what I need, she thought foggily, and with a bit of luck Jake would be gone by the time she was finished.

With unsteady hands she stripped off every stitch of clothing, and, turning the taps on full blast, she stepped into the shower stall. Her whole body went rigid with shock at the first touch of the icy spray. Katy turned her face up to the water and gradually, as it streamed through her hair and over her shivering body, she regained control of her befuddled brain. She had no idea how long she stood under the freezing torrent, until a loud banging on the bathroom door penetrated her consciousness.

'Katy,' he roared, 'if you are not out of there in two minutes I am breaking this door down.'

Jake! She groaned. Was she to be spared nothing? She had hoped he would leave, but obviously he had followed her as far as the bedroom. She was in no fit state to cross swords again with him, but it looked as if she had no alternative. Turning off the shower, she stepped out of the cubicle, and, wrapping a fluffy white towel around her soaking wet hair, she rubbed her shivering body dry.

'Thirty seconds.' The deadly intent in the two words was unmistakable.

Quickly Katy slipped on a large towelling bathrobe and tied the belt firmly around her waist. A quick look in the bathroom mirror stopped her dead in her tracks. With her face scrubbed clean of make-up, and her hair firmly confined beneath the towel, she looked nothing like a pin-up; instead she looked like a very ordinary and rather frightened young woman.

'Ten seconds.' The sound galvanised her into action, and with a shrug of her slender shoulders she walked to the door and unlocked it.

'Oh!' The surprised exclamation left her lips before she could prevent it. Jake was standing by the large double bed and appeared to be in the process of discarding his clothes. Her heart slammed against her breast, her eyes widening as she saw he had removed his jacket and tie, his shirt was unbuttoned almost to his waist, and he was deftly removing the gold cuff-links from the pristine cuffs of his shirt.

Her gaze lingered helplessly on his muscular chest, and for a moment she had a terrific urge to run her fingers through his black curling body hair, to feel once again his firm tanned flesh beneath her hands. Involuntarily she took a step forward, the sheer animal magnetism of the man drawing her like a magnet. She raised her eyes to his, and froze at what she saw there.

There was a menacing controlled violence in his dark eyes that she had never seen before. For the first time she recognised his Italian heritage. He scrutinised her slender form with a savage ruthlessness that made her feel she was naked. Instinctively she pulled the belt of her robe tighter, and stiffened her spine.

'What the hell do you think you are doing?' She went on the attack, swallowing hard on the knot of fear that rose in her throat. Just how much whisky had the man drunk? she wondered, noting the odd glint in his black eyes.

'Talking with you never got me anywhere, Katy. I am going to do what I should have done years ago: take you to bed and make love to you until you are so damned senseless that you will agree to anything.'

All her instincts told her to run, but whether it was the after-effect of the wine or just sheer bravado she didn't know. Instead she watched him walk towards her—and what did he mean, 'agree to anything'?

The hand that reached out and lifted her chin was firm, but she forced herself to ignore the pressure of his fingers on her jaw, and, raising her eyes to his, she arched one perfectly shaped brow derisively. 'Honestly, Jake, darling, I had no idea you could be so dramatic.' She forced a laugh. 'But the evening is over now, and I think you'd better leave.'

Her casual response infuriated him, and for a few timeless seconds Jake looked capable of murder. Then in a low voice harsh with anger he grated, 'Oh, no, Katy, darling,' mimicking her words, then his hand closed on the lapel of her robe and ripped it open, not with violence but with a cold, premeditated resolution. 'It is only one-thirty and I have paid until two.'

Katy's bravado vanished in an instant; she raised one hand to push him away, and with the other tried to grasp the edges of her gaping robe, but he was too fast for her. With consummate ease he caught her wrists and pinned them behind her back in one large hand. 'Let go of me, you great brute!' she screeched.

'No!' The implacable negative was snapped out like a gunshot as his other hand deliberately untied the belt around her waist.

She was terrified. The musky male scent of him stirred her senses, reminding her of emotions she had thought long since dead. Belatedly she started to struggle, but she was helpless against his superior strength. He towered over her, large and unyielding, and her futile exertions only resulted in her robe sliding off one shoulder completely.

His dark eyes slid ruthlessly over her exposed breasts, down to her narrow waist, the flat plain of her stomach, the nest of soft golden curls at the apex of her thighs, then slowly over her shapely legs. She was virtually naked, and heat flooded through her at his blatant cynical appraisal of her trembling form.

'You're being ridiculous, Jake. Please... let me go.' She tried to reason, and wasn't above pleading for her release. She was more terrified than she had ever been in her life.

'Ridiculous! I was once, you lying little bitch. My God! You even made me feel guilty with your apologetic plea that you were too young for commitment. You wanted to see the world. When all the time you thought I was a womanising rogue. I waited two years for you. Give her time to grow, let her have a fling with people her own age, I told myself, and then you laughed in my face. Well, by God! Tonight you have laughed for the last time; you're grown up now. Your exploits are well-known, and tonight it's my turn for some of the action. You sure as hell owe me. You used me to get rid of your cumbersome virginity and then I wasn't worthy to touch your saintly body. What a joke... Now any man can have you for a price...' His dark eyes narrowed on her pale face, and his hand curved around her bare shoulder as with a jerk he pulled her hard against him.

He was wrong, so wrong; she had to tell him before this went any further. She raised her face to his, and the merciless expression in his dark eyes seemed to burn into her soul. He was pitiless in his rage and looked capable of anything. Her body was trembling so much that she could hardly control it. Nervously she ran the tip of her tongue over dry lips. 'Please——'

He did not let her finish. His dark head lowered and he brought his mouth down with punishing ferocity upon hers, forcing her lips apart, plundering the soft inner tissue until she tasted the sweetness of her own blood on her tongue. It was no lover's kiss, but a kiss of angry, savage possession.

His hand at her back, holding her wrists, forced her against his muscled thighs. She felt the hard potency of his masculine arousal, and an unwanted flood of sexual awareness consumed her trembling body. She tried to resist the shattering sensual impact, but when his other hand slid from her shoulder to cup one full breast a shaft of arrowing excitement seemed to shoot from her breast to her loins.

She whimpered low in her throat, and as though it was a signal Jake had been waiting for his mouth eased on hers, and his hand released her wrists to curve around her waist and bend her back over his arm.

Katy knew she could break free, but his fingers had found the pert pink tip of her breast and plucked gently, bringing it to a tight hard nub of aching desire. His hand roamed tauntingly from one creamy mound to the other, and she was delirious with the pleasure he gave. His mouth grazed her throat, and her back arched in willing anticipation of the feel of his mouth on her sensitive breasts.

Her slender arms of their own volition slid up and under his open shirt to cling shamelessly to his broad shoulders.

Jake growled deep in his throat and swung her up into his strong arms. His mouth spread a trail of fire down her throat and lower to capture one hard nipple between his teeth.

It had been too long since she had been in a man's arms. Jake's arms. Since she had felt the fierce pleasure of sexual arousal, and Jake had seduced her utterly. She made no demur as he laid her on the bed, and came down beside her, pulling her robe free from under her body. His mouth found hers and this time she parted her lips willingly, welcoming, wanting his kiss and more, much more.

He lifted his dark head, and, supporting himself on one elbow, raked her naked body with black glittering eyes. With one long finger he gently outlined her love-swollen pouting lips. 'You're beautiful; a total wanton, but beautiful. How could any man resist what you offer so freely?' His hand trailed lower to cover her breast. But his throatily voiced comment acted like a douche of cold water on Katy's overheated senses.

She stared up at his handsome face. He was studying her naked body like a connoisseur of fine art. She recognised the gleaming triumph in his dark, passion-filled eyes, and turned her head away. How could she have been so stupid? Such a push-over?

Her eyes lighted on the bedside clock, and in that instant she knew what she had to do.

'Not freely, Jake, darling,' and before he could register her words she had slid off the bed and picked up her robe. If it had not been so shameful she could have laughed at the look of stunned amazement on his flushed face. 'It is after two o'clock, Jake. Your time is up.' He thought she was a whore, so she might as well act like one. Gathering every scrap of self-control she could muster, she sauntered across to the door and walked out.

She had stepped about two paces into the sitting-room when Jake caught up with her. He grabbed her arm and flung her round to face him. 'How could you do that to me?' He caught her hand and forced it down to his thighs. 'You can't leave me like this, you bitch.'

Brazenly she faced him, though she was shaking inside with fear and repressed sexual desire. 'Well,' her hand trembled on his arousal, but she forced herself to continue, 'do you carry five hundred in loose change? I don't take credit cards.'

For one terrifying moment she thought he was going to hit her. He raised his hand, his black eyes spitting fire, then abruptly he shoved her away, and, turning on his heel, went back into the bedroom.

Katy slowly crossed to the long velvet sofa and sank into the soft cushions. She had caught a glimpse of something so terrible in his eyes as he had turned from her. She knew without a doubt he would never bother her again.

She watched as he returned, shrugging on his jacket. She lowered her head, unable to stand the disgust, the look of icy contempt in his dark eyes. She was unaware of his step towards her, or the flash of anguished regret that contorted his handsome face. She only heard the closing of the door as he walked out of the suite without saying a word.

Katy's head fell back against the soft cushions and a long-drawn-out sigh escaped her. Jake had gone, thank God! She had just put on the greatest act of her life, and he had fallen for it. She should have been pleased, but despairingly she recognised that one minute longer and she would have collapsed at Jake's feet, begging him to take her.

Moisture glazed her huge green eyes and slowly a tear trickled down her soft cheek. Self-pity was an unenviable emotion, but tonight she could not help herself. Why? Why? her heart cried. Of all the men she had ever

met, Jake and only Jake was the one man to awaken the
sensuous side of her nature to a fever-pitch of wanting.
Tonight had taught her a hard lesson.

For years she had convinced herself she hated Jake,
but sadly now she was forced to face the truth. It was
not love; it couldn't be—she despised the man—but the
chemistry, the want, the explosion of feelings his presence
aroused in her was never going to go away.

It was something she was going to have to learn to
accept and live with. Choking back a sob, she lifted her
hands and rubbed the tears from her eyes. Rising from
the sofa, she walked into the bedroom. Her heart
squeezed in a spasm of pain as her glance rested on the
rumpled bed, the image of herself and Jake barely fifteen
minutes ago, locked in a passionate embrace, vivid in
her mind.

She turned her back on the bed and the memories it
invoked and, picking up the towel that had dropped from
her hair earlier, she moved to the dressing-table and sat
down on the low stool. Determinedly she began rubbing
her hair dry. Massaging her scalp had a therapeutic effect
on her overwrought nerves, and, finally dropping the
towel, she picked up a comb and with grim determination began combing the damp tangle of her hair into
some semblance of order.

Thinking clearly for the first time in hours, she began
to question Jake's motive in bidding for a dinner date
with her. True, if he had asked her for a date in the
conventional way she would have refused. But any time
in the past two years he could have seen her at any of
the well-publicised shows and parties she attended.

He was a very powerful man with an entrée in all levels
of society. He knew her well enough to know she would
never have caused a scene. So why go to the trouble of
bidding for what he must have known was going to be

a very public date with photographers in attendance? It didn't make sense...

Jake Granton was notorious for avoiding publicity; he was rarely mentioned except in business articles in the serious newspapers, and it was rare to see a photograph of the man or any mention of his private life in the popular media. God knew, she had looked!

In four years Katy had only seen one article about Jake in an Italian glossy. Her full lips quirked in the semblance of a smile. She had spent the whole evening in her hotel room in Rome, trying to decipher the same article with her limited knowledge of Italian. What a fool! she thought wryly.

Finally she admitted to herself she had never succeeded in tearing Jake out of her heart. It had been a self-delusion. She had run to France and stayed there. Developing a different career had helped her pretence.

Abruptly she stood up and crossed the room to the wide bed. No more, she vowed silently; as of now her game-playing was over. Next week she hoped to start working as a designer. Jake and all that had been between them was over, and she had to face the fact and get on with her life.

She shrugged off her robe, and, pulling back the covers, she crawled into bed. As for Jake, she had nothing to fear from him any more. The glimpse of pure unadulterated hate she had seen in his eyes, minutes before he had left, told her more clearly than words that the last part she had played had been her best and most convincing.

CHAPTER THREE

KATY buried her head in the pillow, but the slight, lingering fragrance of Jake's cologne clung to the crisp cotton covers, forcibly reminding her of their earlier lovemaking, and more—all the other moments she had shared with Jake...

She stirred restlessly on the bed, finally turning to lie flat on her back, her green eyes staring blankly at the ceiling. Her mind spun on oiled wheels, preventing her from finding the oblivion of sleep. Small cameos of her past stirred flickering images in her brain.

Six years old and running around the huge grounds of the family home in Cornwall. A massive granite four-square structure built on the hills above the little harbour of Fowey, a few miles from the china clay works that had been the foundation of the family business almost two hundred years ago. She had been a happy child, living in the huge house with her mother and grandfather. Her father had returned from the factory in London most weekends, and sometimes her mother would take her to London to stay in the elegant town house.

Looking back down the years, Katy could pin-point the exact moment things had begun to change. She had been ten at the time. Her father had returned home unexpectedly late one Thursday evening. She had awoken to the sounds of angry voices—her parents' and also her mother's friend Auntie Fiona's. The following morning the young Katy had run to her parents' bedroom, needing reassurance, only to find her mother on her own; her father had been occupying a separate bedroom.

From then on her father's visits were fewer, and Katy's trips to London stopped. When her dad did visit the talk was all about sending Katy to boarding-school. Her beloved grandfather died six months later, and at the funeral her parents had another row. The landlady of the local pub, the Bird in the Hand, cried at the graveside, and her mother had been disgusted. Katy could hear her father's voice even now.

'Mother has been dead for twenty-five years, for God's sake. He was a normal, healthy man, something you wouldn't understand, given your views on sex.'

Thinking about it now, she wondered for the first time if maybe her mother had been frigid. It was no excuse for the behaviour of her father but it might go some way to explain it.

By the end of the year Katy was a boarder at St Oswald's School for Young Ladies in the heart of Yorkshire. It was there that one of the older girls pointed out to her a photograph of her father and a young woman leaving a London club in one of the tabloid newspapers beloved of the school caretaker. Suddenly everything that had happened in her home over the past year made sense: her father was a philanderer and her innocent trust in home and family was badly damaged.

On the day of her mother's death in a car accident the police called at the factory, looking for her father. He was missing—abroad with one of his lady-friends. By sheer coincidence, Jake Granton had chosen that day to visit the factory. At the instigation of Mary, her father's secretary, Jake agreed to travel to Katy's boarding-school and break the news to the fourteen-year-old child.

He took her home to Cornwall and stayed rather than leave her with only the housekeeper for company. Jake supported and comforted her, until her father finally arrived on the morning of the funeral. It was Jake who explained her father's absence and told her she was too young to understand the emotions between adults and not to judge her father too harshly. At twenty-six, he appeared a confident young man, but near enough her generation to be comfortable with, so she tried to believe him.

Jake talked about his own mother's death a few months previously; he understood her feelings. He had only recently returned from Venice, where he had been acting as his father's envoy and settling his mother's affairs.

Katy sighed inwardly. It had been a peculiar trick of fate that had brought herself and Jake together—the death of two women within months of each other.

In Venice Jake had discovered a great-uncle had left him the shares in Meldenton, and on investigating had unearthed the story behind the holdings.

In the Second World War Grandfather Meldenton had been posted to Italy and there he had saved the life of an Italian man, Gianni Luzzini. After the war, when Grandfather Meldenton had needed capital to refurbish the London factory that had been badly bombed, Gianni, whose family had manufactured glass in Venice for centuries, had insisted on helping him. In return Gianni had reluctantly accepted a thirty per cent holding in Meldenton. Grandfather Meldenton's pride would not allow him to take the money as a gift.

Over the next twelve months Katy had been delighted to receive postcards from various parts of the world from Jake, but it had been the following summer before she had seen him again.

Her father had taken her to his new villa in Marbella and introduced her to Monica, his new bride, an attractive redheaded woman at least twenty years younger than himself. He'd also told Katy the house in Cornwall was to be sold—Monica did not like the country. Their home from then on was to be in London. Katy had been horrified, but Jake had turned up and with a few carefully chosen words had persuaded her to accept her father's marriage. From then on, Jake had always visited when Katy was at home.

Katy groaned and turned over, burying her head in the pillow. She wondered how she had ever been so damned gullible, such a fool, but at fourteen she'd had an outsize crush on Jake. He was the tall, dark, handsome man of her dreams, and she would have done anything for him . . . and eventually did!

It had been the Easter holiday in her last year at school. She had gone to the villa in Spain, loaded down with books to study for her A level exam. On arriving she had found Jake already in residence. He was convalescing after a skiing accident the month previously. She was horrified to see him hobbling around on crutches with his leg in plaster from thigh to ankle. Her father and Monica stayed for a few days, then left—nursing an invalid was not Monica's style.

For Katy the next two weeks were pure bliss; with only the elderly couple who looked after the villa to chaperon, Katy delighted in looking after Jake. They talked for hours, played Monopoly and chess, and Jake taught her to play backgammon.

It was the backgammon that was her downfall. The last evening of her holiday she was desperate for Jake to treat her as a woman.

Oh, he touched her—an arm round her shoulders, a quick hug, a kiss on the cheek—but she wanted more;

just looking at him made her heart beat faster, her stomach turn over. She ached to be held in his arms and feel his beautiful mouth on hers.

Katy had read about love in books and longed to experience the reality of it with Jake, and that night for the first time she beat Jake at backgammon. She could remember it as though it were yesterday.

Jake lounged back on one side of the long hide sofa, his injured leg stretched out before him, his arm spread along the back of the settee. She had never seen him look more sexy. His dark eyes sparkled as he laughed at her across the width of the low coffee-table.

'Well, Katy, you finally did it. You beat the master, and by my reckoning I owe you five thousand pounds.' They used matchsticks as money, and, chuckling, he threw a handful of matches at her. 'I must be a great teacher,' he opined smugly.

Katy, elated at winning, but sad at the thought of leaving the next day, daringly responded, 'I admit you're a good teacher Jake, but, I wonder, is backgammon all you can teach me?' And, standing up, she moved around the table and sat down beside him on the sofa.

She looked at him without speaking, her green eyes brilliant in the perfect oval of her face. She was wearing a brief self-supporting smocked-top cotton sundress, and as she leaned towards him the front slid lower, revealing the soft full curves of her high breasts. She watched his brown eyes darken as his glance dropped to her breasts, she noted the dull flush spread along his high cheekbones, and all trace of amusement vanished from his expression.

He surveyed her smoulderingly. 'What else do you want me to teach you, Katy?'

Katy felt her heartbeat quicken until it almost deafened her. She moved closer and, leaning over his hard body, she reached her slender arms around his neck. 'A kiss instead of the five thousand you owe me,' she tried to joke.

He moved suddenly, his strong arms folding around her as his hard mouth imprisoned her trembling lips. His kiss was all she had imagined and more. His tongue thrust between her parted lips, the consuming heat he ignited in her sent shock-waves crashing through her body. When he finally broke the kiss she was trembling violently in his arms. Gently he held her head to his broad chest, his hand softly stroking her long blonde hair.

'I know, sweetheart, I know.' The huskily voiced endearment was exciting but oddly soothing. 'You want me to teach you to be a woman, and I will, I swear, but, Katy, I'm almost thirty and you are not yet eighteen; I have to be strong for both of us. For God's sake, you still have some months at school. You must concentrate on your exams, but when they are over I promise I will show you what it is to be a woman.' And, lifting her chin with one hand, Jake stared down into her eyes, his handsome face flushed.

'Damn it, Katy, I should have more self-control,' he groaned. 'You must know the effect your magnificent body has on me.' And, lying over him, her legs between his, she did.

'Yes, Jake,' she murmured throatily.

'At the right time and the right place you are going to be *mine*,' he declared emphatically.

Katy's body flushed with heat at the memory, and restlessly she turned over on the bed. Jake had kept his word, she thought bitterly.

She had finished her exams by the half-term holiday in June, and had gone to the London house for the holiday. Her father and stepmother had greeted her perfunctorily and given her a gold wrist-watch for her eighteenth birthday the following day, and within the hour had left for a weekend party. With only the housekeeper for company, Katy had felt rather deflated until Jake had called.

He'd given her an exquisite heart-shaped emerald pendant surrounded by tiny diamonds on a slender gold chain, and kissed her, declaring throatily, 'Thank God you are eighteen.'

They had spent a wonderful three days together; behaving like tourists, they had visited the Tower of London, taken a river boat from Richmond to Hampton Court, got thoroughly lost in the maze and spent hours just kissing and touching. Playing with fire!

What had happened next was inevitable. Every evening he had left her at the respectable hour of about ten until the Sunday, the last night of her holiday and the housekeeper's night off. She had cooked a light meal of ham omelette and salad for Jake and herself, and then they had settled down on the sofa in the sitting-room to watch television.

The tension, the electric awareness between them that had been brewing all weekend, exploded with the first touch of Jake's lips on hers. There was no doubt in Katy's mind that Jake loved her, and within seconds they had shed their clothes and, naked, in a fever of kisses and caresses, he made love to her with an urgent powerful tenderness, the first stab of pain vanishing in the wonder of his thrusting skilful possession.

Later when he had carried her up to her bed and joined her in it, he made love to her again and said he had something to ask her but only when she had left school. He loved her, but there was no way he would propose to a schoolgirl. She knew exactly what Jake meant, and his avowal of love and fidelity she swallowed whole, never doubting him . . .

Lying in each other's arms, they made tentative plans for the future. Katy had already been accepted by a private college in Paris, along with her friend Anna, but at Jake's instigation agreed to look into enrolling at a London art college.

Jake reluctantly said goodnight and sneaked out of the house as the dawn was breaking. He promised to be back, waiting for her, when she finally left school. The following day she returned to school for the last time, ecstatically happy and with her future assured, or so she thought...

The school prize-giving was the day before the end of term, and Anna's father Mr la Tour had arrived to see his daughter presented with the student of the year award. Afterwards he asked Katy if she wanted a lift back to London with them; there was no necessity for her to stay to the final day and have to catch the train back to the city.

Katy leapt at the chance, and the decision changed her life. They arrived in London very late—almost midnight. Mr la Tour insisted on carrying her suitcase to the door, and waited while she quietly opened it and let herself in.

Even now, four years later, the scene that met her eyes that night still had the power to hurt her. The hall was in darkness, but a thin sliver of light shone through the partially opened study door. She thought her father was still up and had taken a step forward when the unmistakable voice of Jake sounded in the silence.

'Really, Monica, my reasons for marrying Katy have nothing to do with you.'

Katy stopped; she was shocked that Jake had told her stepmother of his intentions before even asking her. But then she realised that Jake had probably asked her father's permission and obviously he must have told his wife. She grinned—Jake's words confirmed her treasured hope. She took another step.

'Shh, Monica, I heard something,' Jake said.

'Jake, darling, don't worry. David has been in bed for hours. I wear him out. But you and I never wore each other out, did we, sweetheart? Remember when we went skiing and never left the hotel for two days?'

Katy froze in horror at her stepmother's words, all her dreams turning to dust and ashes in her breast. With horrified fascination she stared through the partially opened door. She saw Jake's back and Monica's arms curved around his shoulders. She heard her stepmother's voice as if from a great distance.

The throaty laugh. 'You know, Jake, on reflection it is probably a good idea for you to marry Katy; my being your mother-in-law gives us the perfect cover for anything we want to indulge in.'

Afterwards Katy did not know how she got out of the house. All she could think of was Jake and Monica, together. For four years Jake had visited her home, and she had thought it was to see her, and all the time he had been using her blind adoration for him to mask his affair with her own stepmother...

She hailed a cab and instructed the driver to take her to the Savoy, where Anna and her parents were staying. Anna was stunned to see her but listened while she cried out all her horror and pain at what she had discovered. Anna's parents were most sympathetic, and renewed their offer to let her stay with them while she was at college. They were leaving for Paris the following evening, and Katy decided there and then to go with them.

But first Mrs la Tour, with a few well-chosen words, persuaded her to go back to her father's house when she was originally supposed to be arriving home the following day.

'Katy, there is no need to tell what you saw and heard.
You are too young for marriage; you want some fun.
An explanation along those lines will suffice, and save
your pride.'

Katy had done just that. Jake had appeared to be
stunned when she had speedily informed him in front
of Monica and her father what she intended doing. Jake
had insisted on talking to her alone but she had resisted
all his appeals to stay in London, and the arrival of Mr
la Tour had cut short the argument.

Thinking about it now, lying in bed in her lonely hotel
room, Katy recognised that it was only because her emotions had been frozen in shock that she had managed to
carry it off. It had taken her months to get over the pain,
and tonight she had been forced to realise that she had
not really succeeded.

Jake had written to her in Paris, having got her address from her father. At first she'd forced herself to
reply with a few lines extolling her life in France to re-
inforce her explanation for leaving him. But after a few
weeks she'd deliberately composed a 'dear John' letter,
telling him she had met a young student and Jake had
been right all along—he was too old for her.

To her amazement he had replied with an eloquent
letter—he was deeply disappointed, but understood, and
hoped they could remain friends. From then on flowers
had arrived for her birthday and Christmas, plus a few
postcards in between. She was hoist with her own petard.
There had not been a thing she could do about it without
confessing the real reason for leaving him. Two years
later, not long after her first appearance on the cover of
Vogue, Jake had appeared in Paris. She'd had no excuse
not to meet him, but she'd chosen her ground carefully,
arranging to see him at Anna's house along with Anna's
husband and Claude.

She had played the party girl and dashing young model for all she was worth. He had asked about the young man. 'Which one?' she had taunted, while clinging to Claude's arm. Jake had been furious.

But still when he'd caught her on her own he had again asked her to marry him. She had laughed in his face, and told him Claude would not like it.

'And you said I was too old—what the hell do you call him?' Jake had snarled. His rage had been terrible to witness and finally he had stormed off in disgust, calling her nothing better than a whore.

She had never seen him again until tonight, and it was obvious Jake's perception of her had not changed. Perhaps it was just as well, she thought fatalistically. Jake still had the power to hurt her, but only if she let him.

The last few years had given her confidence, and now she perceived herself as a successful, mature young woman, not a naïve young girl. The men she had met in the modelling world had reinforced her firmly held belief that no man could be trusted. Wryly she admitted her father looked a saint compared to some of the men she had met. Yawning widely, she burrowed down under the covers, and finally as the light of dawn flickered across the sky she fell into a troubled sleep.

'Katy, girl, it is good to see you back where you belong.' Her father sighed contentedly and settled back in the big winged armchair, a coffee-cup in his hand. 'Looking at you sitting there, I can't see any trace of Lena Lawrence, the celebrity. I never asked, but do you expect me to call you Lena?'

'No, Dad, of course not.' She smiled and stretched her long jeans-clad legs out in front of her, allowing her head to fall back on the soft cushion of the sofa. It had been much easier than she had imagined, coming back to her father's house, though she had been shocked at the change in him. When she had left he had been a handsome middle-aged man with a slightly thickening waistline. Now he was very much overweight and looked every one of his sixty years.

They had shared a splendid lunch of roast beef, and were now relaxing in the drawing-room with a pot of coffee. 'In fact, Dad, that's what I wanted to talk to you about—Lena Lawrence.'

'I can't pretend I was pleased to see your picture plastered over the hoardings, or the gossip about you in the newspapers, but I suppose it all goes with the territory. I never thought my little girl would be such a great success. It took some getting used to, I can tell you.'

'Well, it's all over now, Dad. Lena Lawrence has officially retired, as from yesterday. From this day forward I intend to be myself: Katy Meldenton.'

'You've retired! At your age . . . !' he exclaimed.

Katy laughed out loud at the look of astonishment on his face, but she quickly sobered when she realised her father was not amused. In fact as she studied his flushed face she got the distinct impression that he was avoiding looking at her.

'You don't want to be too hasty, Katy. There must be a lot of money to be made in your profession. Why, it could lead to films, television—the sky is the limit.'

'Yes, so I've been told, but I already have enough to buy an apartment and still keep some change in the bank. Your trusteeship has ended now, Dad, and, well, I intend taking up my seat on the board of Meldenton.' There was no mistaking the shock on her father's face at her words. 'But more importantly I want a job. I would like to be a designer, as Mum was when you first met her.'

Her father tried to talk her out of the idea, but by the time she left to return to her hotel Katy had won. The following day she checked out of the hotel and took a taxi to her father's home.

Tears sparkled in her large green eyes as she looked around her old bedroom. It was stupid, she knew; as a teenager she had not particularly cared for the large Georgian town house. But now she realised she had missed it. Her bedroom was unchanged—the same single bed, the pretty pink and white flowered colour-scheme she had picked herself. It was all so familiar. She brushed the moisture from her eyes with the back of her hand. How often she had lain in this room dreaming of Jake...

No. She was not going to think of him. That part of her life was over, and tomorrow she was going with her father to the factory, and the start of a new lifestyle.

The Meldenton family business had started with the china clay works in Cornwall in the middle of the seventeenth century. By the middle of the eighteenth century one of her ancestors had decided, rather than just shipping the clay to the porcelain factories of London, he would start up his own factory on the banks of the Thames. It was to be the turn of the nineteenth century before the factory became a reality, and by 1850 Meldenton porcelain ranked alongside anything the Imperial Potteries of Lambeth could produce.

Katy could remember her grandfather taking her to the British Museum, and showing her a flask marked 'Stephen Green, Imperial Potteries, Lambeth' and bearing the cipher of Queen Victoria. It was then he had explained the history of Meldenton. His own father had trained with Green before working in Meldenton.

Katy thought about the past in an attempt to banish her nervousness at the prospect of starting her new job. The next day her father drove the car through the

London traffic with the skill of long practice, and when he finally parked she looked around her in amazement. The factory she had remembered as huge now appeared as a dingy place trapped between two large high-rise apartment blocks.

She turned to her father. 'What happened?' she asked.

'Nothing for you to worry about, Katy. About four years ago I diversified into the construction industry; these are part of the company.'

Katy might have asked more, but her father stopped the car and with almost indecent haste jumped out. Two months later she was to wish she had . . .

The early-morning sun glittered on the Thames, turning the slowly flowing water to a stream of shimmering gold. Katy drained her cup of coffee and replaced it on the window-sill. It was a perfect late-October morning and the leaves on the young trees planted at the front of the apartments were already blanketing the ground in a carpet of orange and red. She had moved into the apartment two weeks ago, having bought it from the family firm. It was in an ideal position—she could walk to work in two minutes.

Work. A contented sigh escaped her. In a brief eight weeks she had succeeded beyond her wildest dreams. The men on the factory floor had passed the odd comment, and at the same time speedily removed one of her advertising posters from the canteen wall. But their curiosity had soon fizzled out when they realised she was serious about her work.

She had persuaded her father to let her try her hand at designing, and he had agreed but insisted she try the other departments as well. The first week, instead of going straight into the office, she had started with one of the decorators in the factory.

The glazed china was decorated by using transfers of ceramic enamel covered with a plastic coating stuck on to backing sheets. The decorator's job was to soak them in water and lift them carefully from the backing, and then skilfully slide them into position on the china, rubbing them down to remove any bubbles.

Katy had made a mess of quite a few before achieving a perfect result. She had been fascinated to see the china after it had been fired again, the coating melted away and the enamel fused into the glaze.

She had spent her second week with a liner, the woman who applied the enamel colour, often as not gold, on the rims and handles of the pieces by spinning them on a turntable and using a shaped brush before the pieces were fired for the last time.

To Katy it had been fascinating, and the hands-on experience had given her a much clearer insight into how her original decorative designs would work. Plus it had earned her the respect of most of the work-force.

She glanced at her wrist-watch and frowned: she was cutting it fine. She picked up the cup and saucer and walked through to the small kitchen. Turning on the tap, she rinsed the china in the sink and stood it on the drainer. She picked up her black leather briefcase and headed towards the front door. Katy hesitated; today was her first board meeting, a new challenge, and, turning, she surveyed her reflection in the hall mirror.

The image that stared back at her was reassuring. Her blonde hair was pulled back into a neat chignon; she had kept her make-up to a minimum—a subtle pink lip gloss outlined her full lips, the barest touch of mascara darkened her long lashes. The grey wool tailored jacket fitted neatly over her shoulders and traced her slender waist. She ran her hands over her hips, smoothing the soft grey fabric of the slim-fitting skirt. The perfect business image, she thought happily, and with a last adjustment to the floppy white bow at the neck of her blouse she turned and let herself out of the apartment.

Her black moderately heeled shoes clicked jauntily on the pavement as she walked the few hundred yards to the Meldenton offices. She did not see the appreciative male stares as her mind concentrated on the meeting ahead. She would have been horrified to know that the Lena Lawrence image she had always considered an act, a game, was very much a reality. The lithe way she moved, her beautiful face and curvaceous body, stopped men in their tracks whether she was wearing a grey business suit or a bikini.

'Good morning, Mary.' Katy stopped at the head secretary's desk. 'Have my father and Mr Jeffries gone up yet?' And with a tilt of her blonde head she indicated the floor above that housed the boardroom. 'And what about John?' John had been the firm's accountant for donkey's years; he was due to retire at Christmas, but he also owned five per cent of Meldenton.

'Still as enthusiastic as ever,' Mary said, shaking her head. 'You could give me time to answer, Katy! Yes, they are all upstairs, drinking coffee and waiting for you.'

'Oh, damn, I didn't want to be last!' she exclaimed and, swinging on her heel, walked out of the office and along the short hall to the stairs.

Thank God Jake Granton wasn't going to be here! She could imagine the smug satisfaction he would have derived from seeing her appear late. But last night over dinner with her father her fear of meeting Jake again had overcome her resistance to mentioning his name, and she had asked her father if Jake was attending the meeting.

Her father had laughed. 'Good God, no. Jake is much too busy to bother with a small company like ours. Why, the dividend he gets from our shares wouldn't keep him in handkerchiefs. Surely you remember, Katy? His father died a while back and now he is the owner of Granton's. In the past few years the bank has gone from strength to strength; he has branched out as a financier, and there are branches of Granton Holdings all over the world. Plus Jake still heads the Italian company. Spends a lot of time in Italy, does Jake.'

'I see,' she had mumbled, wishing she had never asked.

'No, I don't see much of Jake these days, and he hasn't attended one of our meetings in four years. I vote his proxy. We keep in touch by telephone, which reminds me, I'd better give him a ring.'

At the top of the stairs Katy crossed to the large oak doors, her slender hand curled round the polished brass handle, and for a second she hesitated as a question popped into her mind. Why did her father have to ring Jake? He had never said, and she had been so relieved to know she was not going to have to face the man that she had forgotten to ask.

Turning the handle, she pushed open the massive door and, straightening her shoulders, she said a silent prayer that the correspondence course in business management she had followed for the last two years would prove enough to see her through the next hour, and walked into the room.

The hairs on the back of her neck prickled, her eyes met her father's and he looked away: something was wrong. Slowly she looked around the room; the solicitor Mr Jeffries greeted her, she responded, then John did, then her wary gaze was riveted on the fourth man, who stood silhouetted against the window. With the sun behind him she was not able to see his face clearly, but it made no difference. It was Jake Granton... Her heart missed a beat, she blinked, and stared.

'Good morning, Katy, I'm glad to see you have finally arrived. Shall we sit down and begin?'

'Y—yes. G—good morning,' she stuttered. Her legs threatened to cave in beneath her, and without waiting for a second invitation she collapsed in the nearest chair, and, placing her briefcase on the large oval table in front of her, she clasped her hands tightly together in her lap to stop their trembling.

Katy stared as Jake casually walked forward and took the seat at the head of the table. His dark hair was longer than on their last meeting, but the tanned, ruggedly attractive face still wore that mask of cold contempt she remembered so well.

He had not forgiven or forgotten their last evening together. His black eyes returned her look with a glittering remorseless intensity that sent a shiver of fear down her spine.

What was he doing here? And why was he seated at the top of the table?

Her father held thirty-five per cent of Meldenton, she held thirty and Jake another thirty. John the accountant owned the odd five per cent. Surely the place at the head of the table should be her father's ... ? A dozen questions swirled in her brain, but she had not the courage to voice them; her earlier confidence had evaporated with one rapier-like glance from Jake.

The preliminaries on the agenda were over before Katy actually began to take in what was being said.

'Well, gentlemen, I think we can dispense——'

'Just a minute!' Katy snapped, shooting an angry glance at Jake. She was not going to allow him to ignore her presence—she had as much right to be here as he had. More, she thought positively, slowly regaining some control over her trembling nerves.

'Forgive me, gentlemen and lady, or perhaps Lena.' His wolfish smile and poor attempt at a joke were met by laughter from the other three men, but Katy saw the amusement did not reach his eyes.

'Katy will do fine; after all, we are all friends,' she responded coolly.

'Yes, of course. Now may I proceed?' he asked silkily.

The derisive tone was a deliberate insult meant for her. She nodded her head in reply, not trusting herself to speak civilly to him. He reminded her of a sleek black jaguar, a predator waiting to leap on its unsuspecting prey. His sober navy business suit and conservative white shirt could not conceal the powerful muscled body or a certain aura of danger about him. The other men in the room faded into insignificance beside him.

'As I was saying, I think we can dispense with the official agenda. The only question we need to discuss is the financial state of the company and, in my opinion, not *if* we call the receivers in, but *when*.'

CHAPTER FOUR

KATY turned shocked eyes to her father, fully expecting him to tell Jake he was crazy, but as Jake's deep voice droned on it slowly sunk in to her stunned brain that no one was going to stop him. She looked across the table at Mr Jeffries and John, but they avoided her eyes. Were they all mad? She felt like Alice in Wonderland at the Mad Hatter's tea-party, or maybe they had cast her in the role of the dormouse, she thought suddenly. Well, no way. She was going to have her say. Snapping open her briefcase, she withdrew a bundle of papers, and, waving them in her hand, she jumped to her feet.

'Now wait just a damn minute, Mr Granton. I can read a financial statement as well as the rest of you. Meldenton China makes a very reasonable profit. The order book is more than half full, and two days ago I personally lunched with Sheikh Hassan, the Sultan of Marin in the United Arab Emirates. He liked the design I presented for a new state dinner service and the sales department got confirmation of his order yesterday. There is no reason for the company to fold.' She smiled triumphantly at Jake, her green eyes flashing fire. 'I can only suggest you are suffering from a brainstorm,' she ended sarcastically.

Jake was lounging in the large hide chair, one hand toying with the papers on the table in front of him. He looked up at her, his eyes derisively raking her feminine frame with a blatant sexual thoroughness.

Katy could feel a flush of awareness spreading through her body at his insulting scrutiny, and a feeling of help-

60

lessness engulfed her as she stared at him; he looked dynamic and supremely masculine, his dark jacket taut over his broad shoulders. Why was it? Of all the men she had ever met, he was the only one to have such an instant effect on her. She felt a tug on her arm—her father obviously wanted her to sit down. With a wry grimace she resumed her seat.

Jake's grim voice broke the lengthening silence. 'I suggest, Katy,' he cast her a hard, contemptuous smile, 'rather than wasting your superlative talents selling your designs to Sheikh Hassan,' he mocked, 'you should have persuaded him to buy two large virtually empty apartment blocks. I have no doubt with your attributes you could have sold the man sand,' he opined silkily.

Katy fumed at his implied insult, and the chuckles coming from across the table added fuel to her anger. 'At least I am not trying to wreck this company,' she bit out. 'Who the hell do you think you are, telling us what to do?'

In the ensuing silence one could have heard a pin drop. Katy, still furious, looked around the table, and every man avoided her eyes, except Jake. He watched her carefully, his dark gaze threatening, but spoke to her father.

'Shall I tell her, or will you, David?'

Katy turned to her father, and in the next fifteen minutes the bottom dropped out of her world. All her hopes for a new career shattered into a million pieces, as with mounting horror she listened to her father's stumbling explanation.

He had used the land on either side of the factory to enter the property market. With enormous loans he had started the construction company a few years previously; at the time property prices in London and in the Docklands in particular had been booming.

Bad luck, bad timing. Whatever her father called it, the bottom line was that by the time the apartment blocks were completed the market had slumped. Interest rates had doubled, making the loans virtually impossible to pay back, and with only a dozen of a total of eighty apartments sold they had reached crisis point.

Katy recognised the enormity of the problem, but she could not believe Meldenton China had to be sacrificed. Forcing herself to think clearly, and without emotion, she asked quietly, 'In view of the facts, surely only the property company is faced with liquidation, not Meldenton China?'

'The two are indivisible,' Jake said flatly.

Katy shot him a poisonous glance. 'A person could be forgiven for thinking it was your company, the way you have taken the chair, and done most of the talking,' she snapped.

An unholy gleam of triumph glittered in the depths of his dark eyes. 'A person could be right,' he drawled sarcastically. 'I hold the major vote.'

One look at her father's face and she knew Jake was telling the truth. 'How, Dad?' she demanded, shaking her head in disbelief. 'How could you?'

Jake answered for him. 'I think your father has had enough for one morning, Katy, and I know I have. So I suggest we adjourn this discussion until tomorrow.' Glancing around the table, he continued, 'Ten tomorrow suit?' Murmurs of agreement rippled around the table. 'Good.'

Katy stood up, shoving her chair back. She needed to get away, out of Jake's overwhelming presence, and try and make some sense of what had happened. More importantly she needed some answers from her father, who with unseemly haste was disappearing out of the room. How could he have allowed Meldenton to fall into Jake's hands? It didn't make sense. But as she walked to the door Jake's hand on her arm stopped her.

'Wait, Katy.' He drew her to one side, his fingers digging into the soft flesh of her upper arm, as he murmured polite adieus to the other two men.

An odd breathlessness afflicted her as he bent his dark head towards her, for a second she had the impression he was going to haul her into his arms and kiss her. 'Let go of me,' she demanded unsteadily.

'I will, but first I think you and I should have a talk. I can see by the expression on your lovely face that you are itching to chase after your father and badger him with questions he is in no condition to answer at the moment.'

'And whose fault is that, I wonder?' she declared furiously. Jake was an astute businessman with his finger on the pulse of the financial world. He must have known two months ago that the firm was in trouble.

She did not need Jake pointing out that her father had looked like a broken man when he'd left. She had recognised it, and half of her anger was directed at herself, and all her fear, confusion and frustration vented itself in a torrent of abuse against the man in front of her.

'You have stolen his company and trampled his pride in the dust. What is it with you? Some bloody Latin vengeance because——' She was going to say 'because he married your girlfriend' but stopped herself, instead blustering, 'Because I wouldn't obligingly go to bed with you the other night and your masculine ego can't stand rejection, hmm? Well, I still own thirty per cent of this company and I intend to fight you every step of the way.' How, she had no idea, and for a fleeting instant she wondered if she would live to make good her threat.

Jake's face darkened thunderously, and his grip on her arm tightened till she cried out in pain. Abruptly he dropped his hand, but his black eyes burned like living coals. Never had she seen such rage.

'Don't ever swear at me again...or you will pay for that and every other insult you have offered me a hundred times over.' The sibilant softness of his voice was more deadly than anger. 'Sit down.' He indicated a chair and moved fluidly to resume his seat at the head of the table. 'First, I do not own the company.'

Katy's eyes widened. 'But...then what was all the liquidation business?' she burst out. She had been so smug, so self-satisfied with her new job that she had ignored all the warning signs her father had been giving out over the last few weeks. She cringed at her own stupidity. She had moved into her new apartment, and had never even questioned why only half a dozen of the others were occupied.

'Secondly...I do have the majority vote,' Jake continued, ignoring her interruption. 'I own thirty-five per cent—I bought John's shares. As the company accountant he is well aware of the dire state of the firm, and with retirement looming he was more than happy to sell.'

'In that case,' Katy interrupted triumphantly, 'my thirty per cent and father's...' She stopped as Jake's eyes rested almost pityingly on her flushed cheeks.

'Your father owns eighteen per cent. No more. The other seventeen per cent went to Monica in the divorce settlement, and I hold her proxy.' His dark eyes narrowed intently on her flushed face. 'Now are you ready to listen?' he asked mockingly, not bothering to disguise the triumph in his eyes.

At the mention of her ex-stepmother all the angry indignation deserted Katy. Monica! Somehow it came as no surprise to find that woman involved in the mess at Meldenton.

'When did you buy John's shares?' she asked.

'Six weeks ago.'

After the fiasco in the hotel bedroom. It did not surprise her—she had guessed as much: he was out for vengeance. For the first time in Katy's life she really sympathised with her father; he hadn't a chance against such opponents. There was nothing more to be said, and, rising to her feet, she prepared to leave with what little pride she had left.

She searched Jake's harshly set features. 'Listen! I don't see the point.' She returned to his earlier demand. 'I know you can afford to lose what little the shares are now apparently worth without a second thought. So I am forced to conclude it suits you to put the firm in the hands of the receivers. I accept your decision.'

Pride held her head high, but inside she was shaking, and to think this man had twice proposed marriage to her, she thought bitterly. 'You,' she almost added 'and Monica', but stopped herself in time, 'have planned this well,' she accused coldly. 'I trust you're satisfied.'

'Satisfied? No, but I hope to be.' Cold black eyes glittered with a calculating, sinister light. 'I could with the right encouragement be persuaded to advance the money needed to keep the firm afloat.' There was no mistaking Jake's meaning. A flick of his lashes sent his gaze skimming over her assessingly. 'I have a proposal for you.'

The blood drained from her face; she was trembling, her hatred for the man almost choking her. She swallowed hard, and her green eyes flashed at him. 'A proposal from you...I would rather die than marry you,' she vowed, and, turning, she picked up her briefcase, intent on getting out of the room.

For a long moment there was complete silence, then Jake's mocking laughter rang in her ears. What the hell was so funny? She could find nothing amusing in the situation at all. In fact she was on the verge of tears, and if she did not get away from his hateful presence soon she would lose what little self-control she had left.

'You flatter yourself, Katy; I have no desire to marry you. If I marry it will be some young innocent female, not a shop-worn model,' he drawled silkily as his hand closed firmly over her shoulder and spun her round to face him. 'The proposal I had in mind was a way to save the factory and the china clay part of the business in Cornwall. I know you will not want the responsibility of putting so many people out of work.'

Fury at his insult and embarrassment turned her face scarlet. What on earth had made her automatically think he wanted to marry her? Dear heaven, she groaned inwardly, she had forgotten about the employees in her agitation with Jake. Forcing her turbulent thoughts into some kind of order, she tilted her head back and looked at him sharply. At five feet nine she was no midget, but Jake towered over her like some dark avenging angel.

Unease stirred inside her; an inexplicable dread. There was no trace of the laughing companion of her youth in his austere features—she could not read this man at all. But she owed it to the people who worked at Meldenton to hear what he had to say. 'All right, I will listen to your plan,' she acquiesced, swallowing her anger.

'It's quite simple. I will personally purchase the two apartment buildings from the company. This would solve the cash-flow problem, and Meldenton China would operate as it always has.'

Confused, she surveyed him. 'And that's it...'

One dark brow arched sardonically, a ruthless smile curving his sensuous mouth. 'Not quite. I said earlier I had no desire to marry you. But I do desire you, Katy...

In return for saving the firm and your father's good name, you will become my mistress.'

She stared at him, her strained features reflecting her shocked horror. He could not be serious. Her lips parted. 'That is blackmail...' she whispered.

'Call it what you will, Katy, but that's the deal,' Jake responded hardily, not in the least fazed by her condemnation. 'Take it or leave it.' And, withdrawing a card from his inside jacket pocket, he pressed it into her numb hand. 'My address; any time after six this evening I will be available. At nine tomorrow morning I will call the receivers' office. You have until then to make your decision.'

It was unthinkable. Jake meant to use her, humiliate her, so why was she standing like an idiot, listening to him? Her eyes searched his face, looking for some sign, some indication that it was just a terrible joke, but she could see nothing in his expression but ruthless determination.

She shrank back from him, her body frozen with shock and, though she hated to admit it, fear. Fear of herself, because for one brief moment the thought of sharing Jake's bed, his magnificent body, had stirred an unwanted response inside her. 'Why?' she protested thickly as his hands moved around her waist, drawing her towards him.

'Because you're here, available, and you owe me...'

His dark head bent and his mouth moved over hers with determined expertise. His hands slid down her back to cup her buttocks and pull her hard against her thighs. A shocked gasp escaped her and she trembled as the evidence of his masculine arousal pressed against her flat stomach. His mouth quickly grasped the advantage as his tongue thrust savagely between her parted lips, demanding she accept and abandon herself to the sweet torture of his touch.

Desire and disgust fought inside her; a surging tide of excitement swept through her love-starved body. She must not let him know how easily he could reduce her to the wanton he had so often called her, she told herself, but it was a hopeless task. Her body, with a will of its own, pressed against his hard frame; her full lips softened and clung to his. As he held her with one hand his other hand slid inside her jacket, stroking her full breast through the fine silk of her blouse.

'Oops! Sorry.'

Jake let her go abruptly, and for a moment she was hopelessly disorientated—she had not heard her father enter the room. She flushed scarlet, and hastily adjusted her jacket. Jake, damn him, was standing a foot away without a hair out of place.

'Thank God you two are still friends,' her father said with feeling. 'I know I can trust you to look after Katy.'

'Don't be silly, Dad, I can look after myself,' she burst out impetuously.

'Yes, well, maybe, but Jake here is a fine man, and my one regret in this bloody mess is that I didn't seek his help months ago. I'm too far under now to get out, but I know Jake will do the best he can for us.'

For himself, Katy thought bitterly. Was her father really such a fool, so blind, as to trust Jake?

'I promise, David, I will save as much of Meldenton as I can,' Jake said suavely, his dark eyes flashing a brief message of triumph at Katy before he centred his attention on her father. 'And now you must excuse me— I have another appointment.'

Jake stopped, his hand on the doorknob; across the room their eyes clashed, and she saw the knowing smile of masculine triumph in his. He was perfectly aware he could elicit a sexual response from her with one kiss. His dark eyes challenged her to deny him. 'Damn him!' she swore under her breath; she hated him, but she could not hold his gaze and, lowering her head, she pretended a terrific interest in the table-top...

'I'll see you later, Katy. *Ciao.*' And with a casual wave of a hand he left.

With Jake gone, Katy turned jaundiced eyes upon her father. It was obvious he had been hitting the whisky bottle—she could smell the fumes from two feet away. She sighed; he had been drinking a lot over the last few weeks. Another sign of trouble she had ignored.

Suddenly the enormity of what had happened threatened to overwhelm her and she felt moisture sting her eyes. Deep down in some secret part of her she had nursed the forlorn hope that maybe she was wrong about Jake, and he was the honourable man she had first thought him, but she could fool herself no longer.

She crossed to her father and linked her arm in his. 'Come on, Dad, I'll drive you home. We may as well take the rest of the day off.' And, unless she became Jake's mistress, the rest of their lives off, she thought bitterly.

She blamed herself—she should have paid more attention to her father in the past. If only she had visited him more often, if only she had insisted on being involved in the business, if only she had not let Jake and Monica chase her away... 'If only' was the most futile expression in the English language, she thought morosely, and, taking her father's car-keys, she slid into the driving seat of the Jaguar. She waited while her father settled into the passenger-seat, started the engine and drove off.

'I'm sorry, Katy, terribly, terribly sorry. I betrayed your trust, my own little girl, my family.'

Katy listened with scant attention to her father's ramblings, concentrating instead on driving through the heavy London traffic. She breathed a sigh of relief when she finally reached the town house, and parked the car.

'Have a drink with me, Katy. I don't want to be on my own today. A wake for Meldenton China, hmm?'

The defeated tone of her father's voice hurt her more than she wanted to admit, and, scraping up the semblance of a smile, she agreed. Jake's ultimatum was thrust to the back of her mind. For the first time in her life her father appeared to need her. It was ironic that he had to be virtually destroyed and half drunk before admitting the fact.

She followed her father into the study, and stopped, her eyes widening in surprise. Her mother's portrait was hanging over the ornate mahogany mantelpiece. Monica had removed it when she was in residence, and Katy wondered who had replaced it. Surely not her father?

Her father noted the direction of her gaze and with a half-smile he walked to the drinks cabinet and filled two crystal glasses with Glenfiddich whisky. He returned to her side and held out one glass. She took it from his hand and, raising it to her lips, took a large swallow. Dear God, she needed it . . .

'Lydia was a beautiful woman, Katy. You are very like her. She was the only woman I ever loved.'

Katy turned astonished eyes to her father. She had actually been feeling some sympathy for him, but his blatant lies were a bit too much for her to stomach. Walking over to a large leather chesterfield, she sank down into its welcoming depth. She had not forgotten her father's girlfriends, or Monica, his second wife, though he seemed to have conveniently done so, she thought wryly.

She watched him drain his glass, and immediately refill it. Agreeing to share a drink with him had not been such a good idea, and she wished she were back in her own apartment. Her head ached abominably, and the drink on her empty stomach was doing her no good at all.

'I don't suppose you remember, but when we were first married we lived in this house, and we were happy. You were three when we decided the town was no place for a child, and you and Lydia went to my father's house in Cornwall. We were happy there as well, at least for a while. I can remember you running down the path to meet me every Friday evening. I would pick you up in my arms and twirl you around, and you laughed; always you laughed...'

Katy smiled. He was maudlin, but he was right.

'And then she had to meet that bitch Fiona, the artist.'

'Auntie Fiona, I've never seen her in years,' Katy murmured, almost to herself.

'No, by God! I made damn sure of that.'

Katy shot her father a puzzled glance. He was once more filling his glass. 'Don't you think you have had enough?' she prompted.

'Enough? I've had enough, all right, more than any man should have to endure. I caught them, you know.'

Suddenly Katy realised her father was talking about the past in a way he had never done before. He seemed to have forgotten she was there. He was seated at his large oak desk, staring at the drink in his hand, his lips moving, but she had to strain to catch what he was saying.

'It was our eleventh wedding anniversary that weekend. I had felt something was wrong for some time, and I could not understand what it was. So that week I left London on the Thursday. I wanted to surprise Lydia—a long weekend in Paris or something like that.

Whatever she wanted. I would have given her the world if I could. Instead it was me who got the surprise. Lydia and Fiona in our bed together. Another man I might have understood, but a woman...'

Katy's glass dropped from her hand, her mouth fell open in shock, and her green eyes mirrored her disbelief. But one look at her father told her he was telling the truth.

He was shaking his head from side to side. 'I will never understand; never, never,' he mumbled, and once again raised his glass to his mouth.

Katy stumbled to her feet and, ignoring the glass and the spreading tide of liquid on the thick pile carpet, she moved to her father's side. 'Dad, please.' She did not know what she wanted to say; she only knew she wanted to comfort him.

'Katy, I always loved your mother. I still do. I will when I go to my grave, but I could never forgive her. I took other women out, but it was no good; it was as though Lydia had castrated me. And then she died. Monica was good in bed, and for that I married her... Now she has gone and likely the business with her. But I will never regret divorcing that woman.'

'Dad, you don't have to explain to me.'

'Yes, I do, Katy. But I can't find the words to apologise to you. I have lost your heritage, I have failed my father and betrayed our ancestors and our employees. How am I going to face them?'

'Please, Dad, don't worry about that now. Let me help you upstairs; you're tired; you need to rest.' Slowly she helped him to his feet and together they left the room and mounted the stairs. 'Tonight we will have dinner together, and everything will seem a lot better, Dad, honestly.'

'I doubt it, unless Jake can come up with something.'
He turned his head to look at her and she flinched from
the almost childlike appeal in his watery blue eyes. 'Do
you think so?'

'I know so,' she responded with a smile, and watched
until he was safely in the master bedroom.

She went into her own room, and gave a sigh of relief
as she closed the door behind her. She slipped off her
suit and blouse and lay on the bed, her mind whirling
like a windmill, and every blade a cutting one. The full
horror of the last few hours she could barely contem-
plate, but she had to...

A bitter smile twisted her lovely mouth. For years she
had been cool with her father; she had blamed him for
his girlfriends, and indirectly for the death of her mother.
How had she dared pass judgement on him all these
years? He was right to remind her she had been happy
as a child; he had been a perfect father, a proud, happy
family man. He had never lied to her, and she knew he
had finally, in a moment of weakness, told her the truth
about her mother.

A lot of small instances from the past she saw in a
different light in the wake of his revelation. Her mother
and Fiona had always been together, so much so that
the woman had become Katy's honorary auntie.

With a low groan Katy rolled over on the bed and
buried her face in the pillow. It was not up to her to
judge her parents, but she was swamped with guilt at
her neglect and coldness towards her father. She blushed
with shame. God, but she had been a precocious
teenager, passing a superior moral judgement on her dad
when she had neither the experience nor the knowledge
to do so.

Because of Jake she had shot off to France and mag-
nanimously called her father once a week. In the past

four years they had only met three times, and always at her father's instigation.

Two months ago she had calmly walked back into his life and informed him she was going to take up her rightful position in the firm. She cringed at her own conceit. She had told herself that her years on the Continent had mellowed her view, she was a mature woman and was prepared to forgive her father his little peccadilloes.

For a long, tense moment Katy took a good hard look at herself, and she did not like what she saw. She had sailed through life, taking what she wanted, her father always there in the background with support and, when she had first left home, money.

She was his daughter and she had never once considered his feelings until today. Her mother had destroyed his pride in his manhood, but he had battled on the only way he knew how. A psychiatrist could probably explain more succinctly, but Katy could guess how he must have felt.

Today she had listened to her father apologise over and over again, and beg her forgiveness. She should be the one apologising for her callous insensitivity. Her father had dropped enough hints that all was not well with the firm, but not once had she taken him up on them, asked what was worrying him. Secure in her own little game-plan, she had considered no one but herself. Now her father faced the bankruptcy court and all the attendant publicity, the last vestige of his pride stripped away from him.

Getting off the bed, she took off her underwear and slipped her wrap on. She could not let it happen; she owed her father that much. The pride of generations of Meldentons stiffened her spine as she walked across to the bathroom. She would do whatever it took to save

Meldenton China, and if that included being the mistress of Jake Granton so be it.

An idea hit her, and, shrugging off her wrap, she stepped into the shower cubicle and turned on the water. Maybe she could outwit Jake after all. She had money of her own, and a call to Claude in France would get her back into the fashion business. All she needed was a financial institution that was prepared to lend her money on the strength of her earnings as Lena Lawrence, top model.

As she balefully eyed the contents of her wardrobe a wry smile quirked her generous mouth: most of her clothes were in her apartment and all she had left were a mink jacket—a present from her father she had never worn—and a couple of dresses.

She chose the least provocative of the two—a jade silk jersey sheath. Quickly she donned a wisp of a white lace teddy, and slipped the dress over her head. She smoothed the short, slim-fitting garment over her hips and turned to the dressing-table. Five minutes later, with her long blonde hair brushed and rearranged in a neat French pleat and the minimum of make-up gracing her lovely features, she hurried downstairs to the study.

This morning Jake had caught her unawares and unprepared, and she had forgotten the first rule of business: read everything, including the small print. Before attending the meeting she had read only the report on Meldenton China, and ignored the papers on the property company as being of no interest to her.

Jake's revelations had shocked her rigid, and delivered a crushing blow to her confidence, but at last she was beginning to think clearly and she would not make the same mistake again.

She sat down at her father's large leather-topped desk and picked up the telephone. 'Bonjour, Claude.' In rapid

French Katy explained to her friend what she wanted. A new contract at a much higher salary, and as many outside commissions as he could find for her besides. Plus she wanted an answer tonight.

She replaced the receiver, a dark frown marring her smooth brow. Claude had promised to do what he could; he was not too confident, given she wanted a response within hours, but he promised to call her back later.

Picking up her briefcase, she opened it and withdrew a bundle of documents. Two hours later, her eyes gritty from reading, she raised her head as Mrs Thomas the housekeeper walked into the room.

'Excuse me, miss, but will you be staying for dinner?'

'Yes,' Katy replied, trying to smile. Mrs Thomas had replaced the old housekeeper. According to her father, she was a gem, a widow in her early fifties who had lost her home on the death of her husband, and was grateful for a roof over her head.

Katy expelled a weary sigh. After reading the full reports, she wondered if any of them would have a home before long. It was much worse than she had imagined possible, but still, with her savings and her father's personal wealth, the company might be saved.

Over dinner, which Katy barely touched, she outlined her plan to her father. 'So you see, Dad, with your personal fortune and mine, plus hopefully my earnings over the next year or two, we might be able to hang on. The property market is bound to improve.'

'Katy, Katy darling, I don't deserve a daughter like you. You would give me all your money and your future earnings——'

'That's not important, Dad,' she cut him off. 'The company is what matters.' She did not want him getting maudlin again, just when he appeared to have recovered from his earlier alcoholic depression.

'It's no good, Katy. I don't have any personal fortune; at least, nowhere near enough to save the firm.'

'But Grandad left you tons of money...'

'Yes, that's true, but Monica proved to be a very expensive wife—the villa at Marbella, a yacht in the Mediterranean and the accompanying crew, jewels, furs...you name it, we bought it. But I can't blame Monica entirely. It was my own fault. I reinvested shares in higher-yield stock, but unfortunately also higher risk.'

'Oh, no.' Katy could guess what was coming next.

'One black Monday a couple of years ago my fortune was more than halved overnight, and the divorce settlement last year just about wiped me out. I scraped up every penny I could but I still had to give Monica half of my Meldenton shares in lieu of alimony.'

Katy's snort of disgust did not stop him.

'At the time I thought it was worth it to be rid of the woman, and there did not seem much risk involved. My lawyer arranged it all so that Monica could not sell for two years, and then I was to have first option to re-buy them. It looked a great arrangement on paper; in two years I would have sold the apartments, made an enormous profit, and still controlled the firm. Unfortunately I never foresaw the complete collapse of the property market.'

Katy listened with a kind of fatalistic acceptance of her father's speech; his two wives had effectively destroyed him, and she had done nothing to help.

The ringing of the telephone lightened her spirits a little. She rose from the table and, fingers crossed, walked into the hall. She picked up the receiver. It would be Claude, but, short of some miraculous offer, there was no way she could earn enough to pull the firm through.

'*Bonsoir*, Claude,' she answered his greeting, and listened in growing despair to his rapid French. She did not hear the doorbell ring, and when a strong tanned hand closed over hers on the receiver she almost jumped out of her skin. 'Jake!' she exclaimed.

'Thank you, Claude, she has got your message. Goodnight.' Jake, taking the telephone from her numb hand, spoke briefly and replaced it on the rest.

'How dare you? I was talking! That was a very important call,' she hissed finally, recovering from the shock of his unexpected appearance in her home.

'He can't help you, Katy,' Jake said curtly.

Katy stared up into his dark eyes gleaming with mocking triumph. He was right: Claude could not help her; for some reason he seemed reluctant to renew her contract, but how the hell did Jake know? Was the man clairvoyant? she wondered bitterly.

'Claude was not only my employer, but a personal friend of mine, and you have no right to come bursting into this house and snatching the telephone from my hand.' She spoke vehemently, but inside she was quaking.

'I did not burst in, Katy, dear; your very kind housekeeper answered the door and showed me in. As for Claude,' he drawled the name sarcastically, 'I think your friendship with him has just about ended.'

'No way,' she said shortly. Where did he get off advising her on her friends? she seethed. But her green eyes slid over his tall figure, unable to hold his gaze.

He looked wonderful—better than any man had a right to look, she thought helplessly. When it came to dressing Jake seemed to have inherited the Italian male's casually elegant style of dress. A smart navy topcoat lay easily across his broad shoulders—generously cut, it fell to about mid-calf-length. Beneath it he wore a dark dinner suit and snowy-white shirt, and a maroon-coloured floppy bow-tie nestled at his tanned throat. On most men it would have looked effeminate, but on Jake it just looked stunning.

She did not notice her father's arrival in the hall, she was so lost in contemplation of the man standing before her and puzzling Jake's reason for being here.

CHAPTER FIVE

'JAKE, what a surprise! But it's good to see you in my home again. It's quite a while since you have been here, but now the main attraction has returned, hmm?' Her father's knowing wink and Jake's answering grin were not lost on Katy. 'Have you any new suggestions to solve our problem,' her father continued, 'or have you come to take my girl out?'

Katy's green eyes widened incredulously. Was her father off his head? Surely he realised, she thought cynically, the only reason Jake had not been around in months was because Monica no longer lived here, and the last thing Katy wanted was to go anywhere with Jake?

'Yes, David, Katy and I have a late date to go dancing. I thought it might cheer her up; she is far too lovely to be worrying her head about business,' Jake answered smoothly.

A late date, Katy fumed as she listened to the two men chat away as if she were not there. She'd give him late date... How dared he? She opened her mouth to speak, but at that instant Mrs Thomas interrupted.

'Have you finished dinner, Mr Meldenton, because if so I would like to clear away.'

'Sorry, Margaret; yes, thank you, it was a lovely meal as usual.'

Margaret? Since when had the housekeeper become Margaret? Katy's mouth hung open as her gaze slid from one to the other: her father was smiling benignly at the older woman, and the housekeeper looked positively coy. The hall was beginning to feel like Piccadilly Circus.

Circus was the right word, she thought numbly; the whole day was slipping away from her.

'Get your coat, Katy; we're leaving.'

She opened her mouth again to tell Jake exactly what a lying rat he was, and then closed it yet again as her father agreed with him.

'Yes, Katy, you run along and enjoy yourself.'

In the face of so much male persuasion, Katy had no option but to agree and, turning, she walked upstairs to fetch her wrap. Taking the only thing she could find, she flung the mink stole around her shoulders. Her wrinkled suit she would have to come back for some other day, but she had the horrible feeling she was not going to need a business suit for quite some time.

Walking back down the stairs, she wondered how on earth she had ever been foolish enough to let Jake manipulate her into going out with him; but it was too late to back out now.

'You know, Katy, sometimes I almost forget you are not a pin-up any more,' Jake taunted softly as she reached the foot of the stairs, and he moved towards her, circling her waist with one arm. 'In that slinky dress and fur stole you look very approachable,' he murmured silkily.

Katy shot him a vitriolic look. 'Model . . . the poster was a mistake,' she snapped. He was so arrogant, so sure she would be prepared to fit in with whatever he arranged. But her fury went unchecked as Jake arched one dark brow in blatant disbelief, then turned and spoke to her father.

'Goodnight, David, and try not to worry; I'm quite sure everything can be sorted out quite profitably tomorrow.'

'And just how do you intend to do that?' Katy sneered as he ushered her out of the door. 'You may be half-

Italian, but you are not Machiavelli. Even you can't change a few million losses into profit overnight.'

'No, but you and my money can, *cara*.'

She felt colour creeping under her skin as the insolent Italian endearment taunted her. Incredibly in the turmoil of the past half-hour she had actually forgotten for a while Jake's dishonourable proposal, but now it loomed like the sword of Damocles hanging over her head.

Suddenly realising she was staring at him apprehensively, she lowered her eyes, and slid into the passenger-seat of, to her surprise, a white Rolls-Royce. Alone with him, she did not feel safe, and the past day had been too much. She felt physically sick...

'Do you have any preference as to where we go? Or shall I surprise you?' Jake asked suavely and, slipping the car into gear, he pulled out into the road.

'I'd be grateful if you just drop me off at my apartment.' A horrible nausea was rising in her throat, and the churning of her stomach reminded her that she was not immune to the man by her side. He could still make her heart-rate rise alarmingly, and what was more, he knew it.

'No, I said we were going dancing and we will.'

'I can't see why you are so insistent.' She derided, regaining her self-control. 'We have never danced before—in fact, I didn't know you could.'

'There are a lot of things you don't know about me, Katy. But in the next few months I am sure you will learn to know me as intimately as it is possible to know another person. It should be interesting,' he observed, shooting her a triumphant glance before returning his attention to the road.

His suggestive remark silenced her completely, and for the rest of the short journey she sat lost in the turmoil of her own thoughts. Jake was so supremely confident that she would comply with his request to be his mistress that she wanted to throw his disgusting offer in his face. Like Rhett Butler in *Gone with the Wind* but in reverse. Unfortunately she did 'give a damn', and that was the problem. She couldn't bear to see the family firm go to the wall, to see her father a broken man, and Jake knew it...

The supper club in Mayfair was a small, dimly lit, obviously very exclusive watering hole. A discreet word at the radio-controlled door had gained Jake their entrance. Katy could not help a start of surprise as she recognised one of the young royals, dancing with a quite well-known model whom Katy had worked with countless times in the past.

A dark-suited man took Jake's coat, but before he could take Katy's fur Jake was behind her and deftly removing it. His strong hands lingered a little too long on her slender shoulders and it took all of her will-power to repress the shiver his touch aroused. Finally he released her and allowed the waiter to lead them deferentially to a table in a secluded corner of the room.

It was obvious to Katy that Jake was well known here; he had returned the nods and greetings of quite a few people. 'I'm surprised, Jake; I never saw you as the kind of man who would haunt a place like this,' she commented.

'I don't; I'm a member, of course, but actually this is only my second visit in years.'

Katy shot him a cynical smile. Who was he trying to fool? She sat down on the chair respectfully pulled out for her by a hovering waiter.

'I know most of the people here through business,' he qualified as he took the chair opposite and with a brief word ordered a whisky and water before turning his dark assessing eyes on her.

Lost in her own thoughts, she never noticed his look. Jake's personal life over the past few years was a closed book to Katy. But there must have been dozens of women; somehow she could not see him as being faithful to the likes of Monica, another man's wife... Perhaps he liked variety, and was that a bad thing under the circumstances? she mused.

If she did become his mistress, chances were he would very soon get tired of her. He was used to sophisticated lovers; her virtually total lack of experience would soon pale to a man of his taste. God help her! She was actually seriously considering his proposal.

'Champagne for you, Katy, hmm?'

'No, thank you. I'm not in the mood to celebrate; a Perrier water will be fine.' She shook her head in a negative gesture, but more to dispel her traitorous thoughts than in any refusal of the champagne.

'I am inclined to agree with you—I prefer my women sober,' Jake said smoothly, and, turning to the waiter, gave the order.

Katy ignored his provocative comment and looked around the room, anywhere to avoid having to face the man opposite. On a small stage at one end of the room was a trio playing a kind of mainstream jazz, easy on the ears and enhancing the relaxed atmosphere. A handful of couples occupied the circular dance-floor, moving easily to the soft sound of a blues number.

'Would you care to dance?' Jake's voice broke the lengthening silence between them.

'Not really; this was your idea, not mine,' she responded sullenly, and, picking up the glass of water the waiter had carefully placed on the table, she took a long cooling swallow, which went some way to settle her churning stomach.

'But I will not take no for an answer, my dear,' and, rising to his feet, Jake walked around the table and with one hand under her arm virtually lifted her from the seat.

She shot him a startled glance, and she knew by the grim determination in his eyes, the tight line of his mouth, that he would brook no refusal, and his words had not just referred to dancing...

'At least let me put my glass down,' she said caustically, and, giving in to the inevitable, she allowed him to lead her on to the dance-floor.

She raised her right hand as Jake's arm encircled her waist, but he ignored it and swiftly linked his other arm around her waist, pulling her closely into his hard body; she dropped her hand to his chest, her fingers splayed on his shirt front, trying to put some space between them, but her efforts were futile.

Jake chuckled, a dark melodious sound, and with consummate ease slid one hand down to her buttocks, while his other hand stroked up her spine to rest between her shoulder-blades. 'Come on, Katy,' he murmured into her hair, 'don't disappoint me now. Lena Lawrence would never object to dancing cheek to cheek,' he drawled cynically.

Cheek to cheek! That was not how Katy would have described it. Jake held her imprisoned against his hard frame, their bodies clamped together from breast to toe. She felt the hard muscle of his thigh slide between her slender legs as with an amazing expertise he executed a skilful turn. She held herself rigid in his arms, but the heat of his body, his hand trailing an exploratory path up and down her back, sent quivers of awareness down her spine.

'For God's sake, relax,' Jake said bluntly, 'and enjoy the music. I'm not about to rape you on the dance-floor.'

His hand curved up to clasp the nape of her neck and pull her head back slightly so she was forced to meet his eyes.

'I didn't think you were, but let me remind you, I had no desire to dance,' she snapped back quickly, hating the way he smiled sardonically down into her flushed face. 'I'm tired,' she excused curtly.

'Poor Katy,' he taunted softly. 'But unfortunately this is necessary to let the world at large know your new status.'

'What do you mean?' What new status was he talking about? She frowned, knowing she was not going to like his answer.

'Look around you, Katy. What do you see?'

Katy did as he said and she recognised a minister of state, a few captains of industry—the beautiful people.

'Yes, my dear, this is a very discreet supper club where the élite, or the jet set if you prefer, can dine with their friends in the certain knowledge the worst that can happen will be a few lines in the gossip column of the better newspapers. Our appearance here tonight will give credibility to our new arrangement, while informing anyone who may be interested that Katy, or Lena Lawrence, model, has changed her allegiance yet again, and is no longer the live-in lover of the renowned Claude.'

Katy's stricken face conveyed her feelings. She had not agreed to Jake's demand, but he was so certain she would that it made her blood run cold. 'I wouldn't be so sure about that, Jake,' she said through tightly clenched lips. His assumption yet again rankled. She had never been anything but a friend to Claude, even though she had once tempted Jake to think differently, and as for the rumours of her other men, that was all they had been—rumours. But she saw no reason to defend herself to Jake. Let the man think what he liked; she didn't care...

He shrugged. 'Why fight it, Katy? You'll only get hurt.' He gave her a chilling smile. 'I always get what I want eventually, and you will be no exception.'

'No.' She rejected his assertion vehemently, but knew it was a lie. Financially he held all the cards, and physically just the sight of him was enough to arouse fluttering sensations in the pit of her stomach.

He pulled her closer, his hand easing her head down on to his chest and settling his other arm more firmly around her, if such a thing was possible.

'Ah, but, Katy, darling, you want me, almost as much as I want you, and that gives me an advantage.' One hand slid up to clasp the nape of her neck and she felt the pressure of his long fingers on her throat. 'You threw me out of your bed a few months ago, but I think you will not make the same mistake twice...'

'I hate you,' she whispered, but the words were muffled against his shirt front, and if Jake heard them he gave no sign.

Katy wished with all her heart she had not dismissed him so crudely from her bed. She should have been more diplomatic—or, more accurately, not let him in her bed in the first place. He completely confused her, and being held so close to him, his warm male scent enveloping her, did not help her thought processes one jot.

Why was he forcing her to be his mistress? Because her father had married Monica, Jake's girlfriend? But Monica was free now—there was nothing to stop Jake marrying the woman himself. No, the underlying bitterness, the anger she had sensed in him all day, was directed at her. She had attacked the most sensitive part of the male ego when she had insulted Jake so badly, and she had only herself to blame for the mess she found herself in.

'Stop worrying, Katy, it will put premature lines on your lovely face.' The softly spoken words caressed her brow, and her head jerked back in shock.

The damn man could read her mind! 'And we mustn't spoil your investment,' she scoffed, favouring him with a smooth dismissive glance.

Jake chuckled. 'So, prickly Katy, relax and enjoy the dance—it might never happen.' His dark eyes gleamed with mocking amusement, as he added wickedly, 'But I wouldn't lay money on it.'

Katy loved dancing, and wryly she accepted that sparring with Jake was a losing game. She relaxed slightly against him: dancing was safer. For a large man Jake was remarkably light on his feet. While one tune ran into another the soft lights, romantic music, and the seductive warmth of Jake's body all conspired against her better intentions, and as they moved in perfect unison around the floor her body, with a will of its own, melted against him.

The music increased in tempo, and Jake bent low so that his cheek brushed hers. 'Do you want to continue? Or shall we sit this one out?' he murmured huskily.

The sound of his voice and the up-beat music finally broke through the sensuous daze of the past few moments. Katy raised her head to look up into his shadowed face. 'What's the matter, Jake—too old for the modern stuff?' she sniped in an effort to hide how much the intimate body contact between them had affected her.

'Not at all,' he shot back, and before Katy's startled eyes he stepped away from her, his long body moving with sinuous grace to the sound of the heavy beat. 'Come on, Katy, show me what you can do,' he challenged, and, throwing his dark head back, he laughed out loud at her open-mouthed amazement.

Katy accepted his challenge, and for the next few sets she completely lost herself in the music and the seductive invitation in her partner's gyrations.

She was smiling when Jake finally put his arm around her shoulder and led her back to the table. Her emotions were in turmoil, but for a short while she had thoroughly enjoyed herself.

Seated once more, she gratefully picked up the glass of by now rather flat Perrier water and finished it off.

'Would you like another drink?' Jake asked rather breathlessly with a smile.

He can really be quite human, she thought, for an instant the past forgotten. 'No,' she replied truthfully, and seconds later she wanted to take the word back.

Jake drained his glass and stood up, the slight smile vanishing from his handsome face to be replaced with a hard implacable look. 'Good. Then we can leave.'

Katy murmured, 'Well, maybe it's not that late.' But Jake ignored her and, with a firm hand at her elbow, helped her to her feet.

Carefully he wrapped her stole around her shoulders, and with a brief word to the waiter, and the exchange of some money, he led her firmly towards the exit. She was free for a moment as Jake slid into his own overcoat, but she was too tired to move. She stood like a zombie while he said goodnight to the doorman, and once more his arm draped casually over her shoulder as he led her to the car.

Seated inside the luxurious interior, she fastened her seatbelt with a shaking hand. She knew Jake would not leave her tonight without an answer to his proposal. God knew, she had explored every avenue she could think of to help her father, but the closing of the car door sounded like the slamming shut of a prison cell to her tired mind.

Jake was the only viable proposition. She grimaced, dimly aware that he had slipped in behind the wheel and was carefully manoeuvring the Rolls into the light stream of traffic. A 'viable proposition' did not begin to describe Jake Granton.

'Your place or mine?'

The blunt question could not be ignored. Katy glanced at the clock on the dashboard. One in the morning. Wearily she leaned her head back against the seat and closed her eyes for a second. She was both physically and mentally exhausted, and hopelessly ill-equipped to start arguing with Jake. She had to draw on every last bit of energy to respond sarcastically, 'My, such finesse—you do surprise a girl.' She cast a sidelong glance at his rugged profile; his concentration was centred on the road ahead.

'The time for finesse is over, Katy. I tried it before with you and it got me nowhere.' His lips twisted in a grim smile. 'So which is it to be, Katy?' he asked coldly.

'My apartment, of course,' she managed to reply lightly, deliberately ignoring the deeper unspoken question. 'Dancing with you was quite a novel experience, but I'm tired and I want to get home.' She began to rattle off her address.

'I know where you live, Katy,' he cut her off abruptly. 'The time for prevarication is over. I want a straight answer—yes or no. Do you agree to my proposition?'

Katy stared long and hard at the half-shadowed face; it was impossible to read. She shrank down in her seat as a fierce tension gripped her. 'Jake, you said by nine tomorrow.'

She was not ready to accept his cold-blooded proposal, to actually give him the words. To admit she would sleep with him for money, because that was the bottom line. True, it was a fantastic amount of money, but it would confirm Jake's opinion of her, and deep down it hurt more than she would have believed possible.

'Today,' he corrected flatly. 'And a few hours are not going to make any difference.'

Jake was unfastening his seatbelt before she'd even noticed the car had stopped; he reached across and opened hers, and she flinched as his arm brushed lightly against her breast.

'They might to me,' she managed to respond. 'I do have a few ideas of my own to save the firm. They just need a little time to finalise. Claude...' She knew she was grasping at straws, but if she could just put Jake off...

'Claude is a dead loss,' he told her sardonically. 'Haven't you realised yet I am a very powerful man, and a good deal of the international fashion world happens to be financed by my banks? I received a very interesting call earlier this evening. Why else did you think I came to collect you? I had no intention of letting you wriggle out from under.' He smiled triumphantly down into her horror-struck face, amused at the blunt *double entendre* and her startled reaction.

Katy could not believe what she was hearing. 'Claude's firm?'

'Yes, my dear; in fact, your friend has rather a large overdraft.' He confirmed her worst fears. 'Indirectly I suppose you could say I have been paying your rather exorbitant salary for the last few years. As I see it, the only difference in this new arrangement...is that you won't have to work for it.'

This last shock was too much for Katy to take. Numb, she followed him up the steps to the foyer of the apartment block.

'Key.'

Mechanically she searched her small handbag and handed him the key. She said nothing as he took her cold hand in his and led her into her own apartment.

'You're cold. Come here.' He pulled her into his arms, his dark head bent towards her, and his mouth covered hers.

Katy made no resistance; she sagged like a rag doll in his arms as his teeth nipped her bottom lip, forcing her mouth to open to the invasion of his tongue. He plundered her mouth like a man starved of sustenance, but she made no response. The last shocking revelation had been too much for her.

With a muttered oath Jake thrust her away from him, the backs of her knees hit the sofa, and she collapsed on to it.

'As my mistress you will have to do a hell of a lot better than that,' he opined cynically.

Katy raised her head and with a clinical precision studied his dark implacable features. A muscle tensed along his jaw, and she could sense a latent anger seething beneath the surface of his otherwise expressionless face.

Intuitively she recognised he had just given her a way to beat him. She had not been able to understand why he wanted her. He could take his pick of women. But the reason was obvious: Jake could not stand rejection. Years before, after one night with him, she had turned him down and he had never forgotten.

His plan was clear: this time he would have his fill of her and cast her off when he wanted to. But his male ego would not be able to stand a cold woman in his bed, and, the way she felt at the moment, to lie frigid in his arms would be easy.

'Yes, Jake, I accept your proposition.' Slowly she stood up and walked towards the bedroom door. 'The bed is this way.' She felt as though she were standing outside herself, and someone else was saying the words.

She dropped the fur wrap on the bedroom floor, and without looking to see if Jake had followed she removed her dress. She sat down on the edge of the bed and with slow deliberation she peeled off her stockings. The brief white teddy, her only remaining garment, outlined her curvaceous body with a sensuous provocation she was totally unconscious of as she stood up and pulled the covers back before sliding into bed. Only then did she look across the room.

Jake was standing in the doorway, his black eyes gleaming with angry puzzlement. She had a hysterical desire to laugh. What was he waiting for? A written invitation?

How strange: she felt nothing for him, she who had worried about loving him... Her green eyes watched him coolly as he crossed to the bed. He shrugged off his topcoat, jacket and tie. She watched with detached interest as he removed his shirt. His hands were at the buckle of his trousers when she spoke.

'Just one thing, before you go any further.' She noted the stiffening of his shoulders, and again stifled the desire to laugh. Was he worried she would change her mind? He had nothing to fear. 'I need your word of honour you will save Meldenton, before you get into this bed.'

It was so simple that she did not know why she had worried. He considered her a woman without morals, and, where he was concerned, he was right. She no longer cared a hoot what he thought of her.

He turned to stare down at her pale face. 'You have my word, Katy.'

'Thank you,' she murmured, and closed her eyes. She felt the cold air as he lifted the covers and slid into bed beside her. It would soon all be over. But in that she was wrong...

Instead of the savage onslaught she had been expecting, Jake leant over her and pressed a light kiss on her forehead; then, sliding one arm under her, he lay back down and drew her loosely against the warmth of his large body.

She noted he was naked, but it had no effect on her. She lay passive in his hold, waiting for whatever he wanted to do, secure in the knowledge she was past feeling anything for this man. The realisation that his bank financed Claude, and was therefore indirectly responsible for her success, was more than she could bear. He had destroyed what little pride in her achievements she had left. He had won, but in a way so had Katy.

Finally she could lie in his arms, breathe in the scent of him, and feel absolutely nothing. He had killed the last lingering traces of her teenage infatuation with him. He was not even worth hating, she told herself. Indifference destroyed a relationship much quicker than hate.

'I'm not a monster, Katy. I realise it has been a hell of a day for you. You're worn out—go to sleep.'

Her smooth brow creased in a frown. Jake, comforting her—what was he playing at? Of course! He always managed to have the last word, she thought caustically. Then the deep even sound of Jake's breathing told her he was asleep. Not at all what she had expected. Still, he was paying anyway, she thought fuzzily and, yawning widely, within minutes she was asleep.

The bright morning sunlight assaulted Katy's eyes and quickly she closed them again. A nagging worry touched the edge of her consciousness. Suddenly she sat up in bed, her huge green eyes wide with horror and confusion. She turned her head, the imprint in the pillow next to her confirming her worst fears.

She groaned and collapsed back down on the bed, flinging a slender arm across her eyes as if by some miracle she could block out the previous night. She must have been mad... The sound of running water coming from the bathroom told her Jake was still around. How could she face him?

'Good morning, Katy. I trust you slept well?' The amused mockery in his voice set her teeth on edge. He knew damn fine how she had slept, curled up warm and safe in his arms.

'Yes.' And from some inner well of courage she turned her head and looked at him. 'Thank you,' she mumbled reluctantly, unable to deny he had behaved like a perfect gentleman.

He strolled over to the bed, wearing only a towel, slung low on his hips; with another towel he was briskly rubbing his hair. A blush spread from her toes to her face; he was so magnificently male, all golden tan and rippling muscle. A few drops of water glistened on the dark curling hairs on his chest, and Katy had to fight down the urge to lean forward and lick them one by one.

God, what was happening to her? she groaned inwardly, tearing her eyes away from him. Where had her frigid resistance gone? The indifference of last night? She could never be indifferent to Jake in a million years. She must have suffered a mental aberration to believe otherwise.

He frowned down at her 'No need to thank me. I haven't done anything...yet.'

The threat in his tone was explicit. She forced herself to look at him. She was a mature woman. Jake believed she was sexually experienced, and to appear as a blushing child this morning simply because they had slept in the same bed was ridiculous, but that was how she felt.

She bit her lip, her hands clenched under the covers, as she fought to present a sophisticated image. Jake, by his restraint last night, had proved he was not exactly desperate for her body. Her assumption that he was after revenge was obviously correct. If she had any hope of retaining her pride when she eventually escaped him he must never know how truly vulnerable she really was.

Her mouth dropped open in shock as, without a shred of embarrassment, Jake dropped the towels and moved around the room, picking up and putting on his scattered clothing. She couldn't tear her hungry gaze away from him. He moved with a lithe grace, even when doing such a mundane chore as dressing. His legs long and muscular, his hips taut... and so very much a man. Ashamed of her erotic thoughts, she felt a scarlet tide of embarrassment burn from her head to her toes.

He paused as he zipped up his trousers, and glanced around the room as though he were seeing it for the first time, which in a way he was. A disdainful grimace pulled down the corners of his mouth and, sitting down on the bed to pull on his socks, he remarked, 'This place is too small, Katy.' He turned his head, his dark eyes impersonal as he noted her hands firmly gripping the covers under her chin. 'You still look tired; beautiful, but tired,' he amended, his glance lingering on her face, the dark circles under her wary green eyes. 'Stay in bed this morning and then spend the rest of the day packing. I have a lot of business to catch up on; yesterday was pretty much a wasted day. So I'll send the car round for you about four. Introduce yourself to my housekeeper, and with luck I will be finished at work about seven. Say, dinner seven-thirty. Mrs Charles knows what to expect— she has looked after me for years.' He rattled off his orders as though he were speaking to his secretary.

Katy could not believe her ears. Yesterday had been the most traumatic day of her life and for him 'a wasted day'. The nerve of the swine! He was all hard-headed businessman. He dismissed her beloved apartment as though it were a slum. Anger bubbled up inside her, overriding her intense awareness of the man.

'Now wait a damn minute!' There was no way she was going to follow his orders like some mindless bimbo.

'For God's sake, Katy, don't start being difficult. I'm going to be late for my nine o'clock appointment as it is.'

'You are?' she squeaked, and with a brief glance at the bedside clock she registered it was eight-thirty. 'And what about me? I also have to go to work, and as for moving in with you—forget it.' And, flinging her legs over the opposite side of the bed, she grabbed her robe off the chair and slipped it on.

A hard hand spun her around as she made for the bathroom, Jake's fingers firm around her upper arm. Dark eyes glittered sardonically down at her.

'The whole point of keeping a mistress is that the said lady will always be available to wait on the pleasure of her master, not the other way around, my dear Katy. You no longer need to work. So toddle off back to bed and I will see you later.' And with a mocking grin he propelled her towards the bed. 'You need your beauty sleep. I will take care of the business.'

'No! You're crazy if you think I will give up work just for the dubious pleasure of sharing your bed,' she flung back at him contemptuously.

'I can assure you there will be nothing dubious about the pleasure you find in my bed, Katy, darling,' Jake promised silkily, while his fingers bit into her flesh, drawing her slowly and inexorably closer into the warmth and power of his tall frame.

The tension sizzled in the air. They stood like two protagonists in a judo match, neither one prepared to back down. Jake's dark head swooped, and his mouth covered hers in a hard, demanding kiss. By the time he lifted his head Katy was sagging against him, all resistance gone.

'I'm sorry I don't have time now, but tonight will be different. Now be sensible, Katy; do as I say, and I will see you later. I will settle everything with your father; you have nothing to worry about.' And before she could respond he had swung on his heel and left...

CHAPTER SIX

KATY dipped a lavish handful of scented crystals into the water, and, shrugging off her robe, stepped into the bath. She sank gratefully down beneath the fragrant foam, her head resting lightly against the inbuilt soft-cushioned rest.

She was a teeming mass of quivering nerves and her brain seemed to have taken a holiday. It was all Jake's fault. He had walked out earlier without a backward glance, convinced she would obey him, and unfortunately, now she had time to think, she was fast reaching the conclusion that he was right.

She loved her apartment; it was the first place she had owned, and the thought of sharing it with Jake was abhorrent. When they parted, which was a foregone conclusion, she would still have to live here. There was no way she could sell it—her lips twisted in an ironic smile—that was for sure...

Already Jake had ruined the master bedroom for her; she would never be able to sleep there on her own without thinking of him, not after last night. She would have to use the second bedroom, and if he stayed here in no time at all his presence would permeate the whole place. Perhaps moving to his apartment was the best idea. At least then she could walk away from him when the end came...

It never occurred to her to question her own acceptance of his proposal. Instead she told herself, it's a job like any other. She had made a success of modelling, gone on to make a success at designing. Being a mistress should be simple in comparison. As for her work, she had every intention of staying on at Meldenton, and there was not a damn thing Jake could do about it. He might be able to arouse her sexually. *Might?* Who was she kidding?

Jake had been devious. He had deliberately allowed her to sleep, and her body, relaxed at last, had recovered somewhat from the shocks of the previous day. He was clever, very clever. But when he had kissed her this morning she had been like putty in his arms, even while she hated and despised him as a manipulating pig of a man.

With a disgusted snort she picked up the soap and washed herself all over, rubbing vigorously, as if by some magic she could rub away his touch, the lingering scent of him on her skin. Finally satisfied, she stood up and stepped out of the bath, her decisions made.

Briskly drying herself with a large fluffy towel, she draped it back over the towel-rail and walked naked into the bedroom. She would move in with Jake. It might only be for a couple of weeks, she told herself as with brisk efficiency she withdrew underclothes from a drawer, and an elegant black and taupe patterned wool shirt-dress from the wardrobe. Ignoring the tiny devil inside her that whispered that he was what she had always wanted, she quickly donned her clothes and applied the minimum of make-up.

She was going to work and the meeting this morning, whether Jake liked it or not. She wasn't such a fool as to take him at his word. Katy fully intended to make sure he kept to his part of the deal, and she would not believe it until she saw it down in black and white, before witnesses.

Finally she was getting some business sense. She smiled bitterly at her reflection in the mirror. While Jake was getting probably one of the most expensive mistresses in the world...

There was no sign of her nemesis as she joined her father and John in the boardroom. She did not know whether she was relieved or disappointed. She hid her flustered thoughts by greeting her father effusively.

'Daddy, darling, you're all right after yesterday? No hangover, hmm?' And, leaning over where he sat, she pressed a soft kiss on his round cheek.

'Good morning, Katy, love, and no, I don't have a hangover. In fact, I feel better than I have in months. Jake was on the phone earlier, and our troubles are over. He will be along in a minute, but I can tell you the gist of the deal. Jake is buying the apartment blocks. So I can concentrate on what I do best—making fine china— and I promise you now, Katy, I will never again branch out into something I know nothing about.' Pushing his chair back, her father stood up and pulled her into his arms. Under the cover of giving her a big hug, he lowered his head and murmured, 'And please, Katy, forget my drunken rambling about your mother. She was a wonderful lady.'

Katy had to swallow on the lump that rose in her throat. Her father was so happy. It was in his eyes, his bearing, and she knew he would never have mentioned anything about her mother, except yesterday he had been under such terrible pressure. As he stood back and looked down at her she forced herself to smile. 'I'm delighted everything has worked out, Dad, and I never believed you anyway,' she lied softly.

'Good morning. I see you're all waiting for me.' Jake breezed into the room. 'My apologies, but I had a rather late night with a lovely lady, and overslept.' His dark gaze settled on Katy, and she itched to knock the stupid grin off his face.

Before she could respond he had crossed the room and pulled out a chair. She noticed he had been home to change, and his navy pin-striped suit only served to enhance the aura of energy and power that was such a natural part of his make-up.

'Close your mouth and sit down before you fall down, Katy. You look rather fragile this morning.'

'Thanks to you,' she muttered under her breath, furious he had caught her staring at him.

For the next hour Jake was all business, and reluctantly Katy was forced to admire the way he outlined and explained his reorganisation of the firm. He talked figures with John until her head rang in her efforts to keep up with them. Finally he pushed his chair back and said, 'Right, I think that's everything, and the vote is a mere formality——'

'We still have to have one,' Katy interrupted. 'And I also want to see everything you've outlined in writing.' He was not going to bamboozle her today as he had yesterday.

'But of course, Katy.' He didn't bother to hide the derision in his voice as he added, 'Raise your hands, all those in favour,' and negligently lifted his hand.

'Really, Jake, there's no need,' her father said with a brief chuckle. 'I know what a great personal favour you are doing for me and Katy.'

'Put your hand up, David; it's a man's lot to humour the women in their lives,' he responded with a smile for her father.

Katy felt a complete idiot, but still she raised her hand; she couldn't back down now.

'The ayes have it,' Jake drawled, tongue in cheek. 'And now, I'm afraid, I must dash.' Scraping his chair back, he stood up. 'I have another appointment. I'll be in touch, David.'

Katy sat, her face bright red and her green eyes spitting fire. She felt like a five-year-old suitably chastised by the adults, and as for her father, almost licking Jake's boots, she wanted to blurt out just how much of a false friend the man was. She opened her mouth to speak, but bit back the words as her eyes clashed with Jake's.

He walked around to where she sat, his smile one of mocking amusement. 'You, Katy darling, I will see tonight, hmm?' He wasn't asking but telling her; the deal was struck, and she had no escape. His dark head swooped and he planted a hard kiss on her lips. 'Till later.' His action in front of her father stamped her as his possession clearer than words.

She sat where he had left her, still trying to recover her scattered senses; one touch of his lips and she lost all will to fight him. Her father spoke.

'It makes me very happy to see you and Jake together again, Katy. I always thought you should have married him years ago, but still, better late than never.'

'What? Oh, yes,' she mumbled. Only Jake was not offering marriage this time. He had asked her twice before. Perhaps she should have married him years ago and ignored his affair with her stepmother. In the intervening years none of the men she had dated had aroused the least sexual interest in her; only Jake had the magic touch where she was concerned.

With a sigh she looked around the empty boardroom. There was no point in sitting here—she had work to do, and, getting to her feet, she gathered up her belongings and stuffed them in her briefcase.

She walked down the stairs and along the hall a couple of minutes later, once more the cool businesswoman. Tomkins, the head of sales, accosted her before she reached the design office.

'Great success yesterday, Katy, thanks to you. The Sheikh has dealt with this company for over fifty years, but he was seriously tempted by Wedgwood until you came along with those new designs. You have done a great job.'

Katy smiled briefly at Tomkins, the compliment lifting her spirits. Designing was something Jake could not undermine as he had her modelling career, she thought more cheerfully. With a lighter step she wandered into the studio she shared with Mike Lasty.

She looked around the large pleasant room over-looking the Thames, the huge plate-glass window flooding the space with light. Mike was at his desk in one corner, his head buried in a book.

He was a man in his fifties, and had been with the firm for years, but he obviously wasn't overloaded with work, Katy thought wryly. She had grown to like him, and it always amused her the fascination he had for PG Wodehouse and Jeeves.

He spent hours reading the same books over and over again, and more than once she had seen him drawing cartoon figures of the characters.

'Working hard, Mike?' He jumped in his chair and dropped the book.

'Katy, I wish you wouldn't creep up on a man. You almost gave me a heart attack.'

She smiled; Mike had confided to her that his secret ambition was to get a cartoon strip published in the newspapers. So far he had not got around the copyright issue; privately she thought he never would...

Her drawing-board was a state-of-the-art white and chrome contraption, and gratefully she sat down in the matching white chair, the familiarity of her surroundings easing her troubled thoughts. She turned to Mike. Her performance at the board meeting had seriously dented her confidence, and she badly needed some more reassurance.

'Mike, before I came here to work, who designed the new china?'

'I did, of course, with the help of young Bob, when I could drag him away from chatting up the girls in the factory.' His friendly features relaxed in a broad grin. 'But since you arrived I'm almost superfluous. Your enthusiasm and talent far outstrip mine. I can remember your mother when she first worked here; she was good, but you are great. This old studio has got a new lease of life. Why, even my cartoons are looking better!' he joked.

His kindness and obvious sincerity made her eyes blur with tears, and, brushing her eyes with the back of her hand, she swallowed hard. 'Thanks, Mike. You're a nice man,' she said, trying to smile.

'No trouble at the board meeting?' he asked gently, noting her luminous green eyes. 'I've heard some unpleasant rumours, and I would hate to start looking for another job at my age.'

'The meeting was a great success. Your job is secure,' she reassured him.

'That's OK, then.' Mike breathed a sigh of relief and, patting her shoulder, he returned to his corner and his book.

In that moment Katy realised there was no turning back. Tonight she would become Jake's mistress, but with one proviso of her own. She was determined to carry on her work. She loved the place and the people and she no longer had any doubt she was good at her job. Her relationship with Jake in all probability would be fleeting, but her career in design would be a life-long comfort.

She joined Mike and a few other members of staff in a nearby pub for lunch, but the steak and kidney pie she ordered stuck in her throat. She was grateful for the easy companionship of her co-workers, but after lunch she could not face going back to the office, so instead she returned to the relative safety of her own apartment.

She threw her handbag on to a chair, and, kicking off her shoes, she collapsed on to the over-stuffed sofa. She looked around her living-room. In a few weeks she had decorated it with an energy and determination she had never indulged before, and the net result was a pleasant blend of old and new.

Elegant cream satin drapes bordered the windows. Two large satin-covered sofas stood like sentinels each side of the Adam fireplace. A deep-pile carpet in old rose covered the floor, the colour broken by a delicately patterned Chinese rug in front of the fire. A polished mahogany coffee-table delicately inlaid with elm sported a copy of last week's *Cosmopolitan*, plus a delightful arrangement of fresh-cut flowers nestling in a Chinese ginger jar. A warm, comfortable nest to hide in, but not for much longer, she thought sadly.

From France she had brought her collection of pictures. Some were her own, but most she had purchased from struggling artists on the left bank in Paris. As she looked at them dotted around the walls every one revived a memory of happier times—shopping with Anna, or just strolling around on a Sunday afternoon. The vibrant colours, the humorous touches, reminded her of a happy moment, and her friend.

Katy closed her eyes as a spasm of pain contorted her beautiful face. Would she ever get over the death of Anna? She had thought yesterday was the worst day of her life, and nothing could be worse, but she had a sinking feeling tonight might beat it.

The ringing of the telephone interrupted her troubled thoughts. It was Claude, calling from Paris.

The sound of a friendly voice raised her flagging spirits a little. Anna had married Claude's son Alain straight from college. Mr and Mrs la Tour had been posted to the French embassy in Brazil, and Katy had moved in with Claude.

It had created a lot of unfavourable gossip as his wife had not been long dead, but the truth was that Claude's home was a mansion with a dozen servants, and the only relationship Katy had with him was strictly avuncular. They had all been great pals. When Anna had died Katy had drawn a lot of comfort and support from Claude, and she liked to think she had helped him.

He was calling to remind her it was his granddaughter's—her god-daughter's—birthday in a month, and could she get over to Paris for the party? Also, much to her surprise, he told her if she was absolutely sure she wanted to return to modelling of course he would hire her.

Katy gently refused his offer of employment. It was too late. But when she put the phone down she was no longer quite so depressed. Jake was not as omnipotent as he thought. He had not managed to frighten Claude off.

She walked into the kitchen, filled the kettle, and switched it on. Taking a jar of instant coffee from a cupboard, she ladled a spoonful into a beaker. Her lips quirked in a reminiscent if slightly wry smile at the inscription on the mug: '"Lord give me chastity—but not yet." Saint Augustine, 354-430.' Anna had given her the mug as a present only months before she'd died. She could hear Anna's voice, clear in her mind as though she were in the room with her.

'I couldn't resist buying this for you, Lena, after seeing that poster you did, and knowing you live like a nun. It's not natural. Time enough to be celibate when you're old and grey; at twenty-one you should be enjoying life to the full. This will remind you even saints are human.'

Katy poured the water on to the powder and idly stirred the mixture with a spoon. She had laughed at the time, but maybe her friend had been right...

Poor Anna, her life cut short so young when she had everything to live for. She wondered what her friend would have said about Katy's becoming a mistress. She could guess. Anna of the laughing brown eyes and bubbly humour. 'My God, Lena, from saint to sinner overnight. What a way to go!'

Her eyes misted with tears. Dear heaven, she missed not having another girl to talk to, to confide in. She took a deep swallow of her coffee and fought back the threatening tears. She felt more alone than she had ever done in her life.

Just when she had reconciled with her father and recognised how much he genuinely cared for her, there was no way she could allow herself to get so close to him. Jake Granton had seen to that. She must play her part as his mistress, without her father ever finding out the true reason for her renewed friendship with Jake.

She drained her coffee-mug and replaced it on the bench. She heard a ringing in her head, and it was a few moments before she registered that it was the doorbell. With a weary sigh she walked out of the kitchen and down the short hall, and mechanically opened the door. The way she felt at the moment, even a conversation with a door-to-door salesman would be preferable to her own troubled thoughts.

'Yes, can I hel...?' The words stopped in her throat, her green eyes widening in shock at the sight of Jake framed in the doorway.

'Why the shock-horror, Katy? You didn't think I would let you get away with reneging on our deal? I'm not so philanthropic.' His mouth twisted mockingly as he brushed past her and walked into the apartment.

She followed him into the living-room. 'What are you doing here?'

'I have come to help you pack.' And before she could gather her scattered wits he pressed a hard brief kiss on her open mouth before his gaze swept rapidly around the room. 'It doesn't look as if you have started.'

Blankly she looked into his face: his mouth was a hard tight line, and his eyes, half shadowed by thick lashes, were unreadable. 'Pack?' she parroted feebly, desperate to put off her ultimate capitulation. 'You mentioned to-night.' A sharp stab of desire curled her stomach, and she wanted to reach out to him, then the reality of the situation hit her, and bitterness rose in her throat.

'Look at your watch, Katy,' he prompted sarcastically.

She did—where had the day gone? It was almost six. She looked up to see Jake striding out of the room and along the tiny hall to her bedroom. Gathering her scattered senses, she dashed after him and landed slap up against his chest as he turned at the door.

'Throwing yourself at me, Katy?' His strong hands grasped her shoulders and eased her away from him. His eyebrows lifted mockingly. 'There is no rush, my dear, but I appreciate your enthusiasm.'

She opened her mouth to deny it, and his dark head bent, his mouth taking hers. She shuddered beneath the hot forceful passion of his kiss, and only dimly registered his words as he took his mouth from hers.

'I think you had the right idea after all, Katy—why wait?' And, folding his arms around her, he pulled her hard against his taut thighs.

She was made instantly aware of his aroused state, and with a little cry she pushed against his broad chest as the import of his words penetrated her dazed mind.

'No!' she cried. 'I won't...'

His arms dropped to his sides. She saw his face contort, and his fingers grasped her upper arms. She could feel the fierce surge of rage emanating from him, and she trembled. To her shame a wild excitement sizzled through her body even as her mind told her to fear him.

'We have a deal, you and I, and there is no way you are backing out,' he snarled.

'But my job...' The words fell jerkily from her lips, the blazing intensity of his dark eyes intimidating her.

'A mistress does as she is told, Katy, and as for your job, I have checked, and the studio can function perfectly well without you for a while.'

'But——' she began furiously; she had never thought of Jake as an MCP but obviously he was.

'However,' Jake cut in before her anger could erupt, 'if you like, perhaps it can be arranged for you to return to work in a week or so.'

Jake offering a compromise...being reasonable! 'You don't mind my working?' she had to ask.

'No, not if it pleases you, Katy. You have always been a hard worker, I know that, even if I do not approve of everything you've done. In my experience a woman with an interesting job tends to be a more stimulating companion, and I don't want you to be bored when I am not around.'

'I'll pack,' she said stiffly, and strangely it was almost a relief. When she dared to raise her eyes she was surprised by the transformation: Jake's anger had vanished, his handsome features relaxed in a lazy smile.

'Good girl, you won't regret it—I can be a very generous lover,' he drawled softly, and, swinging her around, his hand at her back, he urged her into the room. 'Get packing while I go and get a drink.'

The casual swat on her *derrière* as she stumbled into the bedroom was enough to refuel Katy's anger and bitterness long enough for her to drag a couple of suitcases out of the wardrobe and empty the chest of drawers of most of her clothes. Swearing vitriolically under her breath in both English and French, she stuffed skirts, dresses and shoes haphazardly in the cases.

'Finished?'

'Yes,' she said curtly, not bothering to look up, and, closing the lid of the last suitcase, she snapped it shut. 'But did you have to make it so plain to my father we were——' she could not say 'lovers' '—friends? It's humiliating enough for me without my father knowing as well.' It had bothered her on and off all day.

He was silent for a moment. 'It was never my intention to humiliate you, Katy, but neither will I lie. Your living with me will be common knowledge very quickly, and your father deserves to be informed of the situation. If you had any idea of creeping back and forward to this apartment, forget it.'

He crossed to where she stood, and his hand reached out and stroked her throat, tilting her head up, his fingers tightened on her chin, his eyes narrowing. 'There is something between us, you can't deny it. I can feel the pulse beating madly in your throat, you melt when I touch you, and, God knows, it's the same for me. Our relationship will be no hole in the corner affair. Understand...?'

Tears stung her eyes, she blinked and swallowed hard. She could deny him no longer. 'I've finished packing,' she said softly, accepting the inevitable.

The Albemarle Towers was an impressive building, and Katy's resolve wavered as she stepped out of Jake's car in front of the entrance. Think of your father, the workforce, generations of family pride, she remonstrated with herself as on trembling legs she followed Jake into the foyer; she stood mute as Jake greeted the porter.

'Good evening, Tom,' and, taking Katy's elbow, he eased her forward. 'This is Tom Charles, Katy; he's a miracle-worker—if you need anything at all Tom will get it for you.' He handed the car keys to the porter. 'Park it, Tom, and there are a couple of cases in the boot, please.'

She looked at the old man in the rather colourful uniform, and tried to smile. He was about sixty, and had the face of a beaten-up fighter: his nose had been broken more than once, and the scars around his eyes were an unmistakable mark of his previous profession. 'Hello,' she murmured, her voice husky with embarrassment.

Jake, completely unconcerned, continued, 'This is Miss Meldenton. She will be staying a while. I will give her a key but I expect you to look after her when I'm not around.'

'Pleasure to meet you, ma'am.' He held out a huge paw, and Katy saw her own slender hand swallowed up in it. She flushed scarlet—she couldn't help it.

The lift door closed behind them, and immediately Katy turned on Jake. 'How could you tell that man I was moving in with you?' she blurted furiously. 'I have never felt so ashamed in my life.'

'Really, Katy, I find that hard to believe. I know you lived with Claude—this kind of arrangement is hardly new to you,' he stated flatly.

'But——' she hadn't—not the way Jake meant—but he cut her off.

'And these are service apartments with high security. If I hadn't told Tom who you were you would never get in or out of the building. Mind you, the idea of keeping you as a prisoner in my penthouse does have some appeal,' he drawled cynically. 'It's probably the only way to keep you faithful.'

'Coming from you, that's rich,' she snapped back. The lift stopped and Jake shot her a hard look, but ignored her comment.

'Tom will bring up the cases later. Come on.' And, catching her hand in his, he led her across a deeply carpeted hall to a large double door, the only one on the landing.

Eyes wide, she stared around the huge room. It had a very masculine feel about it. Large bookshelves covered one wall, with a motley collection of ornaments fighting for a place among the books.

Her lips quirked in the beginnings of a smile as she spied an autographed football. Jake had always been mad about the game. A small paperweight of Caithness crystal caught her attention, and she instantly sobered. She had bought it for Jake's birthday years ago.

A large, well-used but excellent quality hide sofa stood one side of the beautifully carved mahogany surround of the big fireplace. A couple of over-stuffed winged chairs were set at the other side with a small table between them. The pictures dotted around the walls were a splash of vivid colour against the overall impression of brown and beige. Jake obviously liked modern art and she recognised a Hockney.

'Welcome to my home, Katy, and allow me to introduce you. This is Mrs Charles, my treasure; she is also Tom's wife. Miss Meldenton,' he introduced formally.

'I'm pleased to meet you, Mrs Charles.' Katy tried a polite smile, but the older lady merely twisted her lips in response—more a grimace of disgust than a smile.

'Dinner is waiting, Mr Granton,' his housekeeper informed Jake, the coldness in her tone making her feeling on the situation abundantly clear, and with a brief nod to Katy she disappeared through the door behind her.

'She's a marvellous cook, so don't upset her,' Jake said bluntly.

'I wouldn't dare,' she responded drily. Jake had made her position in his home very clear, somewhere beneath that of chief cook and bottle-washer.

'Come along, I'll show you around.' He took her wrist, and led her through the big homely lounge to a smaller formal dining-room.

She had a startling impression of scarlet walls and polished mahogany furniture before he ushered her through to an inner hall. Four doors opened off it, but when he threw open the first one with a flourish she guessed it was the master bedroom.

Her steps faltered as she entered the room. A huge king-sized bed with a deep maroon Paisley-patterned duvet dominated the space. The soft silkiness of Jake's voice unnerved her.

'Our bedroom.' He dropped her wrist and gestured with one strong hand to the right. 'Dressing-room and bathroom off. I'll leave you to make yourself at home. I think I heard Tom arrive with your luggage.' Katy shivered as he reached out, his fingers undoing the top button of the shirt-styled dress she had worn all day. He watched her reaction, amusement tilting his wide mouth. 'You probably want to freshen up before dinner,' he said smoothly, and walked away.

Hysterical laughter threatened to engulf her. 'Make yourself at home... freshen up,' he had said. What for? she thought wildly, her gaze fixed on the large bed.

Katy was dreaming. Once again she was eighteen, and Jake, her friend, her lover, was with her. His lips, gentle as wild silk against her skin, trailed warm kisses over her eyelids, the soft curve of her cheek. Her full lips parted in anticipation as he finally reached her mouth. His tongue flicked leisurely against her teeth, stroked the sensitive roof of her mouth, and her own tongue danced round his in a welcoming caress. Her slender arms moved tentatively in a well-remembered path around his broad back, her fingers reaching up to tangle in the soft black hair of his head.

Once more she felt every pore of her skin open with tingling warmth at his touch. The strong masculine hand curved lovingly around her full breast; his teasing fingers plucked at the sensitised rosy tips, bringing them to pebble-hard turgid peaks.

She arched against the hard heat of him as his lips blazed a trail of fire down her throat, and his mouth suckled hungrily at her aching breasts, first one and then the other, until she was dizzy with desire.

His hand slid down over her stomach and across her thighs, taking her nightgown with it. She shuddered as his long fingers stroked across her inner thigh and found the hot liquid centre of her femininity. She moaned deep in her throat at the exquisite pleasure, her nails digging into his flesh. How many times over the years had she had this dream? And always it ended with her awake and alone...

Katy's eyelids fluttered open, the blood singing in her ears. She didn't want to wake up, to lose this ecstasy. 'Oh, Jake!' she murmured.

'Yes, Katy, yes; open for me.' The deep rasping voice vibrated against her lips. 'You want me, you know you do. You are so hot, so moist, so ready.'

It was no dream. She was awake and in bed with Jake. She had to stop him, but as the thought pierced her drugged senses so Jake nudged apart her legs. She shuddered again and again as his fingers teased and tormented her. It was way, way too late to stop him, and, God help her, she didn't want to.

His mouth closed over hers, his tongue fierce and seeking, and her response was immediate. Her body arched helplessly beneath him. She looked up into his dark eyes only inches from her own, and her heart stopped for a moment; the ferocious gleam of unabashed passion and more—a fiercely controlled anger—made her hesitate.

Sensing her brief withdrawal, he growled, 'No, Katy, not this time,' his stormy glance skimming down the length of her as he rolled over and between her thighs. His powerful body trapped her beneath him; she couldn't have moved even if she had wanted to. Dream or reality—what did it matter? She wanted him . . .

Katy could not deny him; his first touch had set free four long years of hunger. She was on fire for him. His dark body hair acted as a tingling abrasive on her oversensitised flesh as his hands roamed at will over her curvaceous body. The hard rigid length of his manhood pushed against her inner thigh, but no further. She ached for his possession, and writhed beneath him, her nails sinking into his broad shoulders in fierce appeal.

Once more his mouth captured her swollen lips with a savage hunger, his weight came down upon her and she was crushed back into the bed, but still he did not take her. He raised his head, his sensuous lips quirked in a wickedly determined smile. 'You will remember this for the rest of your days, Katy,' he grated, masculine triumph edging his tone.

One hand stroked up to the engorged tip of her breast and once more his mouth descended to it. His teeth bit lightly and she jerked involuntarily; she was lost in a wild sensuous game where only Jake knew the rules. He brought her to the brink of pleasure-pain over and over again as he explored every inch of her with a salacious intimacy she had never known was possible. His mouth once more covered hers, his tongue thrusting in a insinuating rhythm, but still he held back. He broke the kiss and raised his head, his black eyes, molten with desire and something more, fixed on her love-swollen lips.

'How many other men have seen you like this, I wonder...' a hard sheen of sweat glistened on his bronzed skin '...have made you feel like this?'

She stared up into his harsh face, and wondered at the bitterness edging his tone. None...she wanted to tell him, but bit back the word. Then his hand touched her intimately again, sending shock waves crashing through her. 'Please...' She closed her eyes; she didn't care what he thought of her. She could stand it no longer, and her hands stroked down his chest, around his waist, and lower over his taut buttocks. Her questing fingers slid down his inner thighs and closed around the male core of him. 'Please,' she begged again.

'I love to hear you beg, Katy; I need to.' His voice was a deep growl of masculine triumph.

She did not hear her own whimpering cry. She pressed hot kisses on his chest, her white teeth finding the small male nipple and biting in a frenzy of need.

Jake caught her hands and pulled them away from him, and drove into her with a fierce savage thrust.

She felt a brief moment of discomfort, but this was no forced possession—she had begged him to take her.

For a moment he was still, and then slowly he withdrew from her.

'No,' she moaned, and suddenly she was clinging to him as he thrust once again, his massive body taking her in a hard fast rhythm that sent her to a shattering climax in seconds. She felt his shuddering release as he collapsed on top of her, his huge frame moving spasmodically, the tortured sound of their breathing the only sound in the sudden stillness of the room.

Later, although how much later she was incapable of knowing, Jake rolled over on to his back, and with his familiar weight gone the cold reality of her situation hit her.

'You're a devious, cold-blooded, callous swine, and I loathe you.' Her voice echoed in the silence. Was it possible to hate and love someone at the same time? her brain pondered as her eyelids closed.

CHAPTER SEVEN

A LONG way off a bell was ringing. Katy stirred, half opened her eyes, and closed them again. She was warm and comfortable and content. The ringing had stopped. It can't have been important, she thought, sleepily snuggling closer to the source of heat.

She came alert with an unnatural abruptness, disorientated until her heart slammed against her ribs in shock as she recognised she wasn't alone in the bed. Jake was beside her, his muscular thigh pressed lightly against her side as he sat up. It had been his movement in answering the phone that had fully awakened her.

His deep voice, speaking in rapid-fire Italian, grated on her over-sensitive nerves. Carefully she eased herself away from him in the wide bed. Her face flamed as the events of the night returned to haunt her.

'Sorry about that, Katy.' The sheets rustled as Jake pushed them aside and flung his long legs to the floor. 'But it was an important call. We are going to have to go to Venice this afternoon.'

It was a repeat of the previous morning, with one significant difference. Katy's huge green eyes followed Jake around the room, mesmerised by the glowing perfection of his naked form, only today she didn't have the consolation of knowing nothing had happened; instead the memory of their passionate lovemaking, her abandoned response, made her whole body burn with shame.

Jake, completely unconcerned, was once again rattling off his orders. 'Mrs Charles knows what to pack for me, so you can take care of your own luggage. You

119

won't need much. I can probably get the business sorted out in a day or so.' He withdrew a pair of briefs from a drawer and straightened up, his glance brushing over where she lay. 'Katy, are you listening?' he demanded, his voice terse with impatience.

'How could I avoid it? You're barking out your orders like a general to his troops!' she retorted, stung by his actions. The lover had disappeared and he was all super-efficient businessman. She had no experience of morning-after scenarios with one's lover, but even she could see Jake's attitude would not warrant a one out of ten. She supposed she should be relieved; her own emotions were in such a turmoil that she was in no state to examine them too closely, and Jake's prancing around naked wasn't helping.

Jake paused at the door of the bathroom. Brown eyes caught green and he sent her a rueful smile. 'A general, hmm? I take your point, we'll talk after I've showered. Stay in bed and I'll bring you a coffee.'

Katy pulled herself up into a sitting position. She spied her rumpled nightdress on the floor and it took a matter of moments to leap out of bed, pick it up and put it back on. Her instinct was to run and hide from Jake, and from herself, but something held her back.

She climbed back into bed and lay on her back, her eyes fixed sightlessly on the stark white ceiling. She had been running for years and it had done her no good. She was back where she had started, sharing a bed with Jake, and if she was honest it was where she had always longed to be.

Last night...she moved restlessly beneath the duvet...she had let Jake make love to her, and afterwards she had accused him of being a cold-blooded, callous swine. Had she really said that to him? Yes. But she knew it wasn't true.

There had been nothing cold-blooded about Jake's loving. True, he was a skilful lover, but there had been desire, passion, in his touch as well, and he had been as hopelessly out of control as she had in the final shattering climax. Reliving the previous evening in her mind, she was forced to admit Jake had not been callous, but in a way quite caring.

They had dined under the disapproving eye of Mrs Charles, and Katy had barely spoken two words to Jake, her thoughts full of the night ahead. She'd had no illusions; she had made a deal, and very shortly Jake would expect the first payment. Fear and a tingling excitement had held her equally in their thrall.

They had retired to the lounge for coffee, and watched a documentary on television. Katy couldn't have said what it was about, the tension in the air blocking her ability to concentrate.

Jake had sat in a brooding silence for about half an hour before telling her he had work to do in his study and abruptly leaving the room. She had breathed a sigh of relief, and when the clock had reached midnight she'd been falling asleep where she sat. Finally she had gathered enough courage to walk to the bedroom . . .

Katy was just beginning to relax under the soothing spray of the shower when she heard the bathroom door open. She jumped out of the shower and grabbed a towel, holding it protectively in front of her.

'Jake, what are you doing?' she squeaked. She knew the answer before she had finished speaking. He had undressed down to his briefs and seemed to fill the bathroom.

'Sharing your shower appeals,' he declared throatily. His brown eyes darkened to black as his gaze swept her virtually naked body.

She stared at him, her legs almost failing her at the fierce predatory look she saw in his eyes. 'No,' she whispered.

'Yes.' One tanned hand stretched out and flicked the towel from her trembling fingers. His eyes followed a trickle of water sliding down between her full breasts. 'You're even more beautiful than I remember,' Jake said under his breath, and his voice hardened as he went on, 'I've waited a long time for this. Last night I played the gentleman for you, but not any more!'

Katy shrank away from him until her back was against the wall and she had nowhere to go. His voice was not the only thing that had hardened, she realised as she dropped her eyes. He was fully, magnificently aroused. 'Get away from me!' she squealed as his hand once more reached towards her. Acting on instinct alone, she knocked his hand away.

'Is this how you intend to keep your side of our bargain, Katy?' His eyes leapt with temper. 'You made a deal, you took the money, you pay the price,' he sneered, adding sarcastically, 'You are protected, I take it?'

Her heart pounded, the blood rushed through her veins, and her skin broke out in sweat. God, no, she wasn't. But to admit as much to Jake... How could she explain her almost virginal fear to him? True, they had been lovers once, but it had been a tender loving in the dark and secret. His hands clamped on her shoulders and he dragged her towards him. His mouth captured hers in a fierce, angry kiss. She tried to push him away, her hands beating against his broad muscular chest.

'No, I can't. It will be rape!' she cried.

Jake raised his head, only the pulse beating furiously in his clenched jaw betraying the enormous effort it took to retain his self-control. 'You're not laying that one on me, Katy. I may have forced you to live in my home, and share my bed, but I have never forced a woman to make love, and I am not going to start with you, but God knows you could drive a man to it.'

He glanced down at her breasts, and Katy folded her arms around herself in protection and shame. She knew what he could see: her nipples, taut and aroused.

'You want me as much as I want you; eventually you will admit it,' he drawled contemptuously and, turning, walked into the shower stall.

Katy scuttled out of the bathroom like a scalded cat, threw on her nightgown and stopped. Where did she go from here? she thought frantically.

Jake strolled into the room, clad in a navy towelling robe. Maybe he saw something in her expression because in a remarkably gentle voice he commanded, 'Get into bed, Katy. I won't hurt you.'

She looked up, their glances fused, and somehow Katy felt her anger and fear drain away.

In the harsh light of day, lying in the bed they had so recently shared, Katy was forced to admit he had not hurt her. He had lain down beside her and immediately gone to sleep.

He was clever, or perhaps devious was a better word, she thought wryly. He was an expert lover with a deep knowledge of women. Later, completely relaxed in sleep, she had slowly awakened to the touch of his lips and the heat of his body, and gloried in his lovemaking.

She loved him...she always had, and she could no longer fool herself. Common sense told her she should hate him, but the past, Monica, faded into insignificance against the pleasure she found in Jake's arms. It was what she'd been born for. She had missed the chance to be his wife—he no longer saw her in that capacity. She understood his character better now; he was more

Latin than she had realised. When he married it would be to an innocent young woman.

With stark clarity she saw it all. Jake would never marry a woman like Monica; a mistress...yes. But a wife? No... And now he considered Katy in the same category. She had no one to blame but herself; she had deliberately given him the impression she was an experienced, sophisticated woman.

A bitter smile twisted her love-swollen lips. She was no actress, but she was about to embark on the greatest challenge of her life. She would play the part of mistress to the hilt. She loved him, and she would take anything he had to offer, but he must never know her real feelings. She recalled Mrs le Tour years ago, advising her to walk away with her pride intact. She would again; when Jake tired of her she would leave with her head held high...

The door opened and Jake entered, carrying a tray loaded with coffee and croissants. His black hair was wet from the shower and combed severely back from his handsome face. He had dressed. A grey suit fitted his broad frame to perfection; the white shirt enhanced the golden tan of his strong throat. She swallowed hard. He looked absolutely devastating...

Her eyes followed him as he walked over and sat down on the edge of the bed. His added weight depressed the mattress, shifting Katy closer to him. The fresh-smelling masculine scent of him teased her nostrils, and her pulse leapt in a thump of sensual excitement.

'Coffee, as promised, Katy,' and, setting the tray down on the bedside cabinet, he proceeded to fill a large cup with the steaming liquid. His dark eyes flashed a sidelong glance in her direction. 'I decided to pamper you this morning: Continental breakfast in bed.' He handed her the cup.

Katy's hand shook as she took the cup. Their fingers touched, and she almost dropped it, the familiar tingling awareness shooting up her arm. 'Thank you,' she murmured, raising her eyes to his.

One dark brow arched knowingly. 'Nervous, Katy? You have no need to be. Much as I would like to leap back into bed with you, we haven't time.'

She gulped a great mouthful of coffee and almost choked. How did he do it—walk into her mind like that...? 'We, you said,' she prompted, ignoring the implication of the rest.

'Yes, we.' And, handing her a plate with a hot freshly baked croissant on it, he deftly removed her cup from her other hand and replaced it on the tray. 'Eat,' he commanded.

She did as she was told, and the crumbly pastry tasted delicious. Katy had eaten very little last night, but now she felt ravenous.

Jake continued, 'I have to be in Venice by tonight, and you're coming with me. I have family and business interests there. That was my grandmother on the telephone—some problem has arisen at the plant. I'm meeting your father in an hour to sign some documents, so I will explain to him why you can't make it to the office for a few days. Let me see; it's Thursday today— a day to sort things out at the factory. We'll have to stop for the weekend. Then we'll probably need to rest when we return. A day in bed maybe!' His brown eyes flashed wickedly down at her for a second as his hand carelessly stroked the length of her leg outlined by the fine cotton sheet. 'Yes, I'll tell him Tuesday at the earliest. OK...?'

Infuriatingly she felt her flesh tremble where his hand had rested on her thigh. Katy fought to crush her involuntary response. Slowly she chewed the last of the croissant, resentment building up inside her with each bite. He hadn't so much as stopped for breath as he'd arrogantly arranged her life. His mocking 'a day in bed' rankled. Was she so transparent?

Her fingers were greasy from the pastry. She looked at Jake. He had the smug, self-satisfied look of a physically replete male, confidently anticipating further pleasure when it was convenient for him...

'OK?' he repeated, his brown eyes shaded slightly with impatience, awaiting her response.

She looked at him. The arrogant swine had not so much as mentioned last night—not even a peck on the cheek. Why was she disappointed? He had spelt out very clearly the duties of a mistress.

'I said, is that OK?' He drew the word out slowly as though he were talking to a child, and Katy saw red.

'Fine, Jake.' She smiled brilliantly into his dark eyes, and, reaching across him, carefully placed the plate down on the cabinet. She turned and deliberately trailed her greasy fingers straight down the front of his immaculate silver-grey jacket. 'Perfect.' She viewed the long dirty streaks with glee, and, turning limpid green eyes up to his, she reiterated, 'Just perfect.'

Katy chuckled. Jake's expression was comical. He looked down at his jacket, up at Katy, then back to the jacket again. Her chuckle turned to a full-blown laugh. Served him right...

'I don't believe you did that.' The puzzlement in his tone set Katy off laughing harder. 'This is a new Armani suit. You've ruined it.'

'Oh, you poor boy!' she managed to drawl between giggles. 'But then a mistress is a notoriously expensive item, and you have to keep her amused.' She collapsed back down on the bed; she felt guilty about spoiling his suit, but it had been worth it for the look on his face, and it had certainly got his attention.

'You little devil!' Jake roared; it was like a volcano erupting. 'Want a laugh? I'll show you laugh!' And, flinging himself across the bed, he trapped her beneath him. 'I seem to remember you are ticklish here, and here.' One hand curved round her side and the other stroked down and around her knee.

'No, no! I'm sorry, truly sorry!' she cried, then laughed.

They rolled around the bed in a hilarious game of catch and tickle. It was as though the years had rolled back and they were young lovers again. Suddenly the laughter stopped and they stared at each other.

An hour later Jake once again sat down on the edge of the bed, a navy three-piece gracing his magnificent body. His dark eyes roamed lazily over the lovely woman lying there.

Huge seductive green eyes stared back at him. 'You're going to be very late, Jake.'

'And whose fault is that?' Dropping a hard kiss on the softly pouting lips, he stood up. 'Witch.'

Jake had dismissed all her arguments against going to Venice with him, and now, after a smooth flight in, to Katy's amazement, Jake's private plane, which he piloted himself, they were now seated in a motor launch, heading for his grandmother's home.

Katy was sitting on the edge of the seat, incapable of relaxing. It was dark, and the lights of the buildings danced in a multitude of colours on the water, but she was unable to appreciate the beauty of her surroundings. She was too tense, and Jake, lounging in negligent ease beside her, his long legs stuck out in front of him, was not helping at all.

She had dressed carefully for the journey, and she knew she was looking good; the winter white wool suit with the black trim was a Claude original. She had teamed it with a plain black silk blouse and matching black bag and shoes.

She had aimed for a smart conservative look, because she was dreading meeting his relatives. It could only be humiliating for her as her place in Jake's life became apparent to them. In fact she could not understand why Jake would introduce his mistress to his grandmother.

'Where is your grandmother's home, Jake? Are you sure she won't object to my presence? I——'

'Stop worrying, Katy,' he cut in. 'We aren't going there tonight in any case. We are staying at the Cipriani,' and, putting an arm around her shoulder, he pulled her back in the seat.

Katy turned her puzzled gaze towards him. 'I understood it was an emergency. You were needed urgently.'

'So it is,' Jake drawled softly, and, tightening his hold on her shoulder, his lips caught and captured hers in a long, drugging kiss. He raised his head, his black eyes gleaming devilishly. 'But I have a much more urgent need of my own,' he murmured the words against her cheek. 'And in my grandmother's house it will be separate rooms and celibacy.' He kissed her again.

'Then why?' Why had he bothered bringing her? she pondered. It didn't make sense.

'Katy, stop with the questions. We have arrived.'

She looked around and saw the landing stage. She began to rise, but Jake pulled her back. 'No, there are people around,' she remonstrated, believing he was going to kiss her again. Instead he took her hand and slid a ring on the third finger of her left hand. She looked down: diamonds and emeralds glittered back at her; it looked very old and very valuable. 'Why do...?' She never finished the question as he kept a tight hold on her hand and led her on to dry land.

'Jake, wait a minute! Why the ring? It looks very expensive. I don't want——'

'Katy, shut up. It is for appearances' sake only. I am well known in Venice and I would not insult my grandmother by introducing her to my mistress. For the duration of our visit you will be my fiancée. As for the expense, it's a second-hand ring for a second-hand woman—very appropriate,' he said curtly.

In her modelling career Katy had stayed in some of the great hotels in the world, but the Cipriani must rank among the best, she thought wonderingly. Situated on Giudecca Island and set in beautiful gardens, it had everything.

Jake, with his hand at her elbow, kept up a running commentary on the delights of the place, a swimming pool and tennis court—the only ones in central Venice— a health studio and sauna, and situated only a brief boat ride from St Mark's Square.

The receptionist treated Jake as an honoured and obviously well-known guest. Katy felt a swift stab of—could it be jealousy? He must have entertained plenty of other women here, she thought balefully, to be so instantly recognised.

The suite the porter showed them to was stunning. Katy, her curiosity aroused, wandered around as Jake dealt with the porter and their luggage. A sitting-room, a bedroom with an enormous bed centred on a raised dais, and a positively decadent bathroom. She had an impression of polished marble, rich fabrics and subtle colours blended to give an ambience of exclusive grandeur.

'Do you want to dine here or down in the restaurant?'

Jake's voice startled her. She swung around on her heel to find him standing only inches away, his dark eyes watching her with a brooding intensity that sent a *frisson* of awareness tingling down her spine.

'The restaurant.' It would be safer, was her first thought.

'Now how did I know you would say that?' Jake drawled mockingly.

'Well, it is a lovely hotel, and I'm sure the dining-room must be marvellous, and I like the idea of getting dressed up...' She was babbling, but could not seem to stop.

Jake took a step towards her, and she looked somewhere over his left shoulder, determined to retain her control. Unfortunately her vision was filled with the very large bed. The bed she would very soon share with Jake, and the thought did nothing to help her poise at all...

'You must allow me to help you get "dressed up".' Jake strung the words out as his long fingers deftly unbuttoned the jacket of her suit while his lips softly pressed to her brow, the tip of her nose, and softly, very softly, down to her generous mouth.

She stood stock-still, her heart pounding in her chest as he dealt in the same fashion with her blouse. Katy told herself to move; she lifted her foot to take a step back but unfortunately her body had other ideas and instead she stepped forward.

'I love this outfit, but I much prefer what it's hiding,' Jake mouthed huskily against her lips as his hands eased the jacket and blouse off her shoulders.

'Mmm,' she said dreamily, her slender arms winding around his strong neck. 'It was one of Claude's favourites.'

'I should have guessed.' The harshness of his words pierced the sensual haze that surrounded her. She stared up at him, her senses registering the thick sound of his anger, and stiffened slightly. His hand covered her breasts, and his mouth found hers with a savage bruising passion that within seconds had swamped her slight resistance.

A primitive hunger, a want, a powerful need swept away any lingering inhibitions in Katy's mind.

Jake, with speed and expertise, stripped them both naked, and in a tangle of arms and legs, touching, tasting, they sank to the floor in a wild passionate coupling.

'Jake!'

'Katy!'

Their cries mingled as their bodies fused and ignited in a mutual explosive release.

Jake lay on top of her, his skin hot and damp against her own, his breath rattling deeply in his throat. Katy, eyes closed, trailed her hands lovingly down his shoulders, his broad back. He might never love her, but he had shown her he wanted her with a fierce passion he could not deny after tonight.

'Did I hurt you, Katy?' Jake rasped throatily. He eased his large frame to one side and, leaning over her, with one hand he gently stroked a few strands of hair from her flushed cheek. 'I didn't mean to.'

Her lips parted in a slow wide smile. 'I'm fine; more than fine,' she sighed, her sea-green eyes lazily lingering on his darkly flushed face.

'God, Katy, we never even made it to the bed.' He shook his head as if to dispel some unpleasant thought. 'I'll make it up to you tomorrow—I'll buy you a whole new wardrobe as a present.'

'That's not necessary.' A present reminded her of her position as his mistress and her quick visit that morning to the family planning clinic; she could only pray the Pill acted immediately. It was some consolation that the

first time they had made love four years ago there had
been no unfortunate repercussions.

Restlessly she moved. 'This floor is rather hard; do
you think we could move?' she queried. Keep it light,
she told herself and teasingly ran a slender hand down
his chest, his stomach.

Immediately Jake stood up and swept her up in his
strong arms. 'Sorry, Katy; I promise you I'm not usually
so impetuous.' And for the rest of the night he proved
it to their mutual satisfaction.

They never made it to dinner; instead at midnight they
rang room-service for champagne and sandwiches.

Venice. Katy stared around her in keen fascination as
the motor launch sped through the water. Jake laughed
at her wide-eyed wonder while pointing out the more
famous monuments. He reluctantly refused to allow her
to stop at St Mark's Square—there was not time—but
promised they would return later.

The private launch sped on. The Grand Canal, lined
with magnificent buildings, meandered its way through
the unique city on the water. Katy's head flew from side
to side as she tried to assimilate the beauty and variety
of the buildings. Imposing palaces, dating back to the
time of the Venetian Empire, jostled side by side with
colourful houses.

The breath caught in her throat as the launch stopped
at a private landing stage in front of a genuine pink-
washed Venetian palace. The long windows were perfectly arched and intricately decorated in handsomely
sculptured plaster and frail lattice woodwork. The delightful romantic balconies reminded her of *Romeo and
Juliet*, although it was the wrong city.

'What is this place?' she asked Jake softly as he helped her off the launch and up a few steps to the massive entrance doors.

'My grandmother's house. The Palace Luzzini.' The door swung open and, hanging on to Jake's arm, Katy walked inside.

She smiled shyly at the old gentleman Jake greeted in Italian, then her eyes widened in amazement as she looked around the enormous hall.

The morning sunlight streamed through lofty windows sparkling like diamonds, and on to a huge, delicate cobweb of a chandelier, the superb glass reflecting every colour of the rainbow. A grand marble staircase curved upwards to the next floor, the stair-rail a masterpiece of the wood-carver's skill.

At the top stood a tall, exquisite-looking lady dressed in an elegant navy wool gown, the colour broken by a fine hand-printed silk scarf in reds and blues draped casually around her neck and over one shoulder. Impossible to tell her age—anything from forty to eighty, Katy thought.

'*Nonna!*'

This was Jake's grandmother! Katy watched Jake rush up the stairs and kiss the older woman on both cheeks. They were both talking at once in rapid Italian. Finally Jake took his grandmother's arm and led her down the stairs. Katy felt a swift stab of envy as she saw the look of love and respect in Jake's eyes. Would he ever look at her like that? Not very likely...

The change in him astounded her. Somehow, although she knew he was half-Italian, she'd always thought of Jake as very British, but in this setting he was transformed into an emotional, thoroughly Latin male.

She smiled warily at the two of them, feeling a bit like a spare wheel, but Jake flung his arm around her shoulders, and, turning a beaming smile on her bemused face, he said, 'Katy, darling, my grandmother. *Nonna*, my fiancée Kathleen.'

Katy responded formally, 'How do you do?' and held out her hand, only to find herself swept against the other woman and soundly kissed on both cheeks.

'Your English formality!' she grinned. 'Please call me Maria, and I will call you Kathleen. I have waited such a long time to meet you that I feel as if I know you already.'

What did the woman mean, 'a long time'? Katy was puzzled, but before she could form a question Jake once more flung his arm around her. She felt like a spinning-top.

'I have to leave now, sweetheart; I will be back this evening, but, don't worry, *Nonna* has strict instructions on how to entertain you.' And, with a brief, hard kiss on her open mouth, he murmured so only she could hear, 'And behave yourself, I will not have *Nonna* upset,' and left.

Three hours later Katy, hot and exhausted, ruefully recognised where Jake got his arrogant autocratic manner from. It was twelve-thirty, lunchtime, and the two women were being ushered out of the door of an exclusive boutique on the Merceria, the expensive shopping street running from St Mark's to the Rialto.

Jake, in his usual devious manner, had got what he wanted. His instructions to his grandmother had been to take Katy shopping. Maria thought it was for a trousseau; Katy knew different, but did not dare say anything. Consequently she had spent all morning getting in and out of clothes. She shuddered to think what the final bill had come to. Casual co-ordinates, day dresses, lingerie, evening wear, shoes, bags, the lot . . . Maria had insisted.

Thankfully Katy followed Maria into the palace, and to a small dining-room, where the table was laid for two. The older woman was inexhaustible, Katy concluded, as over lunch she barely paused for breath.

'You know, of course, Katy, when the tragedy happened Jake was a tower of strength. I don't think I could have survived without him.'

'Tragedy?' Katy queried.

'You do not know? I lost my daughter—Jake's mother—my son and my brother all at once. They were skiing in the Dolomites...an avalanche. It was terrible, but Jake stepped in to look after the family firm. He need not have done; he is more English than Italian, but he has great heart. Carlo, my other grandson, will eventually take over the running of Luzzini's when he is twenty-five in two years' time. So you need not worry that I will be forever calling for Jake when you are married. But now enough of tragedy. You must have a siesta. Tonight we have a grand engagement party. You will wear the green ballgown; I think that was the most beautiful.'

Katy choked on her coffee and stumblingly agreed. An engagement party. God, what a mess... Jake would have a fit.

By eight o'clock that evening Katy was a nervous wreck. She was pacing the corridor outside her bedroom, and had been for the past half-hour. She needed to speak to Jake; fury and fear in equal proportions shadowed her lovely eyes. She looked down at the ring glittering on her finger. An engagement party! The guests were due to arrive any minute. What the hell was Jake playing at?

'Waiting for me, Katy, darling? I'm flattered.'

Her head shot up at the sound of his voice. 'At last,' she sighed with relief.

His dark eyes gleamed appreciatively at the beautiful girl before him. She was a vision of loveliness, her blonde hair piled on top of her head in an intricate twist, a few small tendrils escaping to frame her flushed face. Her gown was mint-green chiffon, the strapless bodice moulding her full breasts like the hands of a lover. The skirt fell in soft folds to float around her dainty feet.

'Where the h...?' Katy stopped, struck dumb by the expression on Jake's face. His brown eyes caressed her and his sensuous mouth parted in the broadest, most beautiful smile she had ever seen. She swallowed hard on the lump that rose in her throat. 'Where have you been?' she breathed softly. 'Have you any idea what is going on? In a few minutes we are supposed to be greeting a horde of guests. An engagement party, for God's sake!' Her voice rose in her agitation. 'Maria has arranged it. What are you going to do?'

'Slow down, Katy. I know. Everything is under control. Give me ten minutes and I will be back to escort you downstairs.'

'But——'

Jake bent and placed a swift, hard kiss on her parted lips. 'Don't panic...' And he strode on down the hall.

At three in the morning Katy, content in the curve of Jake's arm, said goodnight to the last guest.

'A very successful evening, I think we can all agree,' Maria remarked, a satisfied smile on her face. 'If you two young things don't mind I will say goodnight. At my age late nights are reflected on my face for days afterwards.'

'*Nonna*, you love them and you know it.' Jake grinned at his grandmother. 'Thanks for a marvellous party.' And without releasing Katy he bent and kissed the older woman's cheek.

Katy added her thanks to Jake's. It had been a glittering evening. Her earlier panic had quickly vanished as Jake, looking magnificent in a black evening suit, had proudly introduced her to a hundred people. He had been the perfect partner, keeping her by his side all night; he had played the part of doting fiancé to perfection. So much so that after a couple of glasses of champagne Katy had found herself swept up in the make-believe.

'My pleasure, children, my pleasure. Don't be long in going to your rooms. This is not the Cipriani but my home.' The last was said as Maria ascended the stairs.

Katy flushed fiery red. 'My God, Jake, she knows!'

Jake burst out laughing. 'I'm sure she does. That woman knows everything that goes on in Venice. I swear she has a better spy system than the CIA.'

Katy's laughter joined his—she couldn't help herself; the euphoria of the evening was still with her; and, arm in arm, they walked upstairs.

At the door of her bedroom she went willingly into Jake's arms, and the kiss they shared was like none other. It was tender and passionate, speaking, without words, of happiness shared, friendship, and need. Was it love?

'I told you it would be all right, Katy,' Jake murmured, breaking the kiss. His dark eyes gleamed down into hers. 'Trust me. I know what I'm doing.' And Katy, at that moment, believed him.

'Two more nights before we leave,' Jake groaned, the invitation in her sea-green eyes testing his control to the limit. 'I can't bear the frustration.'

Katy's lips parted in a sensuous, purely feminine smile. 'Poor Jake,' she teased.

'Get going, witch.' And with one more brief kiss Jake opened the door to her room, his large hand on her back guiding her in.

Katy heard the door close and the sound of Jake's footsteps retreating along the hall. She hugged herself with pleasure, and in a dreamy state undressed, washed and fell into bed.

Later she was to wonder if Venice had bewitched her. There was no other explanation for her behaviour.

On Saturday Jake set out to show her Venice. It was a whirlwind tour. They travelled along the Grand Canal and Jake pointed out the Campanile, and the Basilica di San Marco, plus the Palace of the Doges from the lagoon. Then they landed and set off walking. Katy marvelled at the beauty of the buildings, and the Bridge of Sighs brought a lump to her throat as Jake explained it originally linked the Palace of the Doges with the prisons and was named apparently from the sighs of the prisoners as they saw the San Marco basin for the last time through the enclosed bridge's small windows.

Hand in hand, they wandered along small alleys and broader walkways. Katy stood in front of the Basilica di San Marco, the very symbol of Venice, and was struck dumb by the sheer beauty of it, the Byzantine façade covered in precious marble, the intricate and exquisite carving of the saints looking as if they would take flight any second.

Jake, completely in tune with her mood, stood silently by her side. Later they had dinner at a small restaurant just off St Mark's Square. They talked and laughed and drank a rich red wine with their huge plates of pasta, and finally they cruised the Grand Canal in a gondola.

Katy had never experienced anything so romantic in her life, and when they finally returned home in the early hours of the morning she told Jake so.

Once more they parted at her bedroom door, and Katy carried the memory of his kiss and the most perfect day of her life on into her dreams.

On Sunday they left Venice. On arrival at London City Airport Jake dashed off to hand in his flight papers, and Katy returned to reality with a jolt...

It had been a wonderful weekend, but a dream. Jake's parting comment echoed in her head.

'God, I can't wait to get you home and out of that suit. Wait here.'

Slowly she removed the diamond and emerald ring from her finger and dropped it in her handbag. The reason for wearing it no longer applied. She was Jake's mistress, nothing more, and for her own peace of mind she would do well to remember that fact. He had dashed them back a day earlier simply to get her into bed. She straightened her shoulders, and when Jake approached she responded to his wide grin with a brief, cool smile.

She was silent on the ride across London. Jake stopped the car outside the apartment, and shot her a quizzical glance.

'Something wrong, Katy?'

'No, of course not. I've had a wonderful trip to Venice, a whole load of new clothes, and I've lied to a nice old lady. What could possibly be wrong?' she queried sarcastically, and reached for the door-handle. Suddenly Jake leant over her and grabbed her wrist.

'Why aren't you wearing your ring?' he demanded icily.

'It's no longer necessary—there are no old ladies to fool here.'

'What about old men—your father, for instance?'

Katy forced a laugh. 'Really, Jake, given my dad's track record with women, I doubt if he could give a damn.'

Jake let go of her wrist. 'Go on up, I'll park the car.'

Katy cast a sidelong glance at his harsh face as she slid out of the car. He caught her gaze and for a second she could have sworn it was a kind of weary defeat she saw reflected in his dark eyes.

CHAPTER EIGHT

KATY put the finishing touches to the delicate drawing in front of her, and, dropping the pencil in the holder, with a contented sigh she sat up straight and stretched her slender arms above her head. Another job completed successfully.

She rolled her head around on her shoulders and wearily looked across the room. The calendar on the wall caught her eye: a photograph of the Alps, but it was the date that caused her to drop her hands to her lap and slouch back in her seat.

Two days to Saturday the first of December, her goddaughter's birthday, and she did not relish the prospect of telling Jake she was going to Paris for the weekend.

She worried her bottom lip with her teeth, her smooth brow creased in a frown. Jake was her problem; she would never understand him in a million years. In the month they had lived together he had confused, irritated, and made wonderful love to her until she didn't know if she was on her head or her heels. But there was no genuine closeness; even in the ultimate act of love an indefinable barrier existed between them.

Oh, they could talk about music, books, theatre or work for hours, all safe subjects. But under the polite surface of the relationship Katy felt the anger and resentment festering, though was incapable of doing anything about it. It was a classic love-hate relationship, she thought bitterly. She loved Jake but hated the way he used her. His sexual expertise overwhelmed her puny efforts to resist him, and she no longer bothered to try. While Jake simply hated her...

He had always avoided publicity like the plague, but over the past few weeks he had taken her out to dine in every well-known restaurant in London. They had been to two first nights at the theatre, a film première with royalty in attendance, a bankers' ball, of all things, and every fashionable nightclub Jake could find.

Their names were now linked in the gossip columns of half the newspapers in the country, and Katy was exhausted. She had come to the conclusion Jake was doing it deliberately, so that when he finally threw her over it would be a very public humiliation. There was no other explanation...

Katy shook her head to dismiss her troubled thoughts. Jake was coming to collect her and that damned white Rolls-Royce hardly blended in with the surroundings. Irritation tightened her full lips as she swung around on the chair to stare blankly out of the window. That was another bone of contention. He hardly let her out of his sight. He insisted on driving her to work. She supposed she should thank her lucky stars he allowed her to come to work. But she didn't feel like it.

Everyone in the factory was perfectly well aware she lived with him. She brazened out the knowing grins and sideways looks because her one source of comfort was her job. At her instigation her father had agreed to the expansion of the limited-edition market.

Katy had just finished a design for commemorative plates for the Chelsea Flower Show next year, and they were good. The buyer at Harrods had been impressed with the samples and ordered accordingly. Her confidence in her work grew day by day. In that one area of her life she was a success, even if the rest of her life was a mess...

The door opened. 'Ready to go, Katy?' Jake's deep, melodious voice vibrated on her over-sensitive nerves.

She jerked upright, her eyes unerringly finding his. He filled the studio with his presence and her heart did its familiar leap in her breast. Resentment burned within her along with a hopeless love for the man. 'You're early,' she snapped.

'I know, but we are going away for a few days, so jump to it, love.' He rubbed his long hands together; whether it was with cold or excitement Katy couldn't be sure. Restlessly he prowled around the room. 'Hurry it. We have to get home and pack.'

'Where to now?' she enquired drily, getting to her feet. There was no point in arguing with him—she had found that much out over the past few weeks. He flattened any objections she made with the thoroughness of a steam-roller, or he made love to her and got the same result.

'Let me guess: dinner in Sicily for the seafood, or perhaps Scotland for the haggis.' She glanced at his handsome face and almost laughed out loud at the puzzled look in his dark eyes. 'No, I've got it!' she exclaimed, flinging out her hand in an exaggerated gesture. 'Lapland for the aurora borealis.'

'Katy, what are you going on about?'

'Nothing; nothing at all,' she said, and, picking up her handbag, she moved towards the door. Jake collected her cashmere overcoat from its peg on the wall and helped her on with it.

His hands lingered on her shoulders; his lips brushed the top of her head. 'Katy, you work too hard; you look tired. What I have planned for the weekend will revive you, I promise. Trust me.'

She stiffened and pulled away from his hold. What she had planned for the weekend certainly would not please him, she thought wryly. Meekly she allowed him to take her arm and lead her out of the building to the car. She watched him walk around the front of the vehicle and slide in to the driving seat. How was she going to tell him? He obviously had plans of his own for the next few days.

Angrily she snapped her seatbelt shut. Why shouldn't she have a weekend off? Even mistresses must be entitled to a holiday...

'Why the hell you drive a car like this I will never understand. It is the most pretentious bloody vehicle.' She took out her frustration on the inanimate object—it was easier.

'But I thought you liked it.' Jake's dark head swung round in amazement.

'Like it? You've got to be joking!' she snorted. It reminded her of a bridal car—the last thing she needed under the circumstances. 'And keep your eyes on the road.'

He stared straight ahead, but Katy was stunned to see his lips quirk at the corners in the beginnings of a smile; then he chuckled, and then he laughed out loud.

'I don't see anything funny in this great monstrosity.' But Jake just laughed all the louder.

'I'll tell you one day, Katy,' he vowed, still laughing.

'Don't bother...' she muttered angrily.

Jake cast her a sidelong glance, all humour gone. His brown eyes assessed her pale face, the resentment bubbling just beneath the surface of her set features. Thoughtfully he drove the car straight into the underground car park of the apartment building. He got out of the car and, walking around to the passenger-door, he solicitously took Katy's hand and tucked it into the crook of his arm.

'There is something wrong, Katy. What's the matter? Don't you feel well?'

If only he knew, Katy thought bitterly. But wait a minute! He had given her the perfect excuse. If she could plead illness perhaps she might just be able to wangle a weekend on her own. 'I'm tired, I guess. We have rather been living it up lately,' she said flatly.

'I have just the cure.' Jake smiled down at her as he ushered her out of the lift and into the apartment. 'How do a few days' complete rest and relaxation in a magnificent hotel set high in the Swiss Alps appeal?'

'What?' It was the last thing she needed.

'Let me explain, Katy. Ever since I was an undergraduate at Oxford a group of us have spent the first weekend in December at the same Swiss resort, the same hotel, for the first skiing holiday of the season. Over the years the numbers have fluctuated somewhat, as people married, had kids, and divorced, but usually there are about a dozen. Not everyone skis, so you could rest, relax, and join in the *après-ski*. So what do you say?'

Katy collapsed on to the sofa and briefly closed her eyes. He looked so eager, a boyish grin curving his sensuous mouth. At any other time she might have enjoyed what he'd suggested, but not now.

'I don't ski, and I don't want to. You go, and I'll visit Dad for a few days. Having Mrs Thomas fuss over me will be a definite improvement on your housekeeper Mrs Charles frowning her disapproval from morn to night.'

Jake sat down beside her, and took her small hand in his. 'It is within your power to change Mrs Charles's attitude,' he said coldly, his good manner gone. With his thumb he rubbed the third finger of her left hand. 'You could wear the ring I gave you, but you chose not to.' He dropped her hand and stood up.

Katy sighed, and stared searchingly up at him. He was a complete enigma to her. She couldn't understand his attitude at all. He looked so aloof, withdrawn; she watched as he walked to the sideboard and poured himself a large measure of whisky. His back was towards her, and she noted the tension in his broad shoulders, but then tension was the norm in their relationship, she thought sadly.

'Maybe you're right, Katy; I can't begrudge you a visit with your father, and a few days' skiing will do me good.' He turned around and raised his glass to her in a mock salute. 'A short break, hmm?'

A wary smile curved her full lips. She couldn't believe her luck. With Jake gone she could nip over to Paris for the birthday party and be back before he knew. She would have to square it with her father, but that was no problem.

Her smile broadened; she felt as if a weight had been lifted off her shoulders. 'Pour me a small martini, please. Be careful on the slopes, Jake,' she teased. 'I seem to remember you breaking a leg once...' The first time they had kissed... God, but she'd been naïve then.

Their eyes met and Katy knew he was remembering the same thing.

'Actually that was the second time I had broken my leg,' he informed her with a grin, his good humour returning. His brown eyes darkened as he placed his glass down on the table, and in two strides he was standing over her, her request for a drink obviously forgotten.

She quivered in anticipation. She knew that look in his eyes so well. He reached down and tilted her head back with one strong hand. 'But it was by far the most memorable occasion, Katy,' he purred as he bent over her, his lips brushing hers in a rare gentle kiss.

She sighed; she was powerless to resist him and her slender arms curved around his neck. Jake swung her up against his broad chest and carried her into the bedroom . . .

Katy let herself into the apartment the following afternoon and walked wearily to the bedroom she shared with Jake. She threw her bag on the bed and kicked off her shoes.

She shivered; the place seemed cold and empty—a wry smile twisted her full lips—probably because it was . . . Jake had left for Switzerland some hours earlier, and with the master gone Mrs Charles had grudgingly told Katy she was off for the weekend.

Katy had been delighted—everything was working out to perfection. She had called the airline and was booked on the evening flight to Paris. Calls to her father and Claude had completed her arrangements, but that had been this morning.

Now she sat down on the dressing-stool and stared with lacklustre eyes at her pale, frowning reflection. A visit to the local family planning clinic to renew her prescription had ended in disaster. She was pregnant. Was there no end to her stupidity? she asked herself.

Jake had, after their first night, sarcastically suggested that of course she was protected and she had confirmed his opinion as befitted her sophisticated image. What a laugh! Hotfoot that morning she had visited the clinic and received a prescription for the Pill. Unfortunately, it seemed, she was too late; the damage had already been done, as today's visit had confirmed.

Katy rested her elbows on the table, her head drooped, her hands covering her face; for long moments she sat, breathing deeply, holding back the tears. What a mess! What a God-awful mess! Then slowly the tears forced their way through her tightly closed eyes. She had been living on the edge for too long, working hard, playing the sophisticated mistress, hiding her real emotions, and this latest blow was the last straw. Her shoulders shook as she gave in to a great paroxysm of weeping.

Crying for herself, for her unborn child, she sobbed as though her heart was breaking, and perhaps it was. She loved Jake and it was tearing her apart. Lying in his arms, lost in passion, she had to guard her tongue in case she let slip the words. In her saner moments she told herself she hated him, he was the rat who had slept with her own stepmother, but nothing seemed to make any difference. One touch of his hand and she was lost.

Her tears slowly ebbed and she raised her head. She had the horrible conviction that the real source of her grief was the fact that, now she was pregnant, she saw little alternative but to leave Jake. She had told herself for weeks that she had made a deal with Jake and she had to stick with it. But deep down a small voice whispered, Excuses, excuses.

Jake's deal with her father had been completed for ages. Jake could not possibly renege on it—the money had changed hands. Katy could if she wanted walk out any time, and there was not a damn thing Jake could do about it. The trouble was her own innate honesty forced her to admit that she didn't want to leave Jake, but now she had no option she couldn't bear the thought of his marrying her just because she had foolishly got pregnant.

'Abortion' was an emotive word. Katy was neither for or against it. She had always held the opinion it was the woman's sole right to choose, but for herself she knew it was a non-starter. There was no way she could abort Jake's child. A despairing sigh escaped her. What could she do? There was not just herself to consider. What about her father? At last they were friends. How could

she deprive him of his grandchild? Running away again
was not the answer...

Abruptly she stood up. Let me get away and think,
relax in Paris with friends. No sooner had the thought
entered her head than she was moving. A quick shower
was followed by a careful application of make-up, slightly
more than usual to hide the signs of her crying jag.

She dressed in the white wool suit Jake had taken such
an aversion to, and, hastily packing a small suitcase with
enough clothes to last her until Sunday plus the parcel
containing the soft cuddly toy, her god-daughter's
present, she called a cab.

When the plane touched down at Charles de Gaulle
Airport Katy sighed with relief, a new enthusiasm lighting
her rather sombre features. She strode confidently
through the Arrivals lounge, a tall, blonde, elegant young
woman, who turned more than a few male heads.

Claude rushed up and swept her into his arms, and in
typical French fashion kissed her on both cheeks.

Katy's eyes misted with tears. 'Claude, it is so good
to see you.' She had not realised just how much she had
missed his companionship. At fifty, he was still a very
attractive man, his steel-grey hair beautifully cut, his
clothes, as one would expect, the last word in fashion
and taste.

'Ah, Lena, let me look at you.'

For a moment Katy was disorientated; she had almost
forgotten her Lena Lawrence image.

'No, Claude, it's Katy now; just plain Katy.'

'*Chérie*, you could never be plain in a million years.
Your bones, even in the grave, will be beautiful.'

'Not for some time, I hope!' Katy laughed at his ex-
travagant compliment, and the tone was set for the
weekend.

Reaching Claude's house on the outskirts of Paris felt like coming home to Katy. She greeted Alain with kisses and a shared slightly sad smile as they both remembered Anna, her friend, his wife. Then all her attention was captured by the dynamic little ball of pink frills, with a shiny black curly topknot, that was her god-daughter and namesake Caterina.

'You darling!' Katy exclaimed, swinging the little girl up in her arms. At two, she was already a perfect replica of her mother, and as the innocent childish eyes smiled into Katy's she had to swallow hard on the lump in her throat.

Saturday was spent with the three adults indulging every whim of the little girl—her second birthday was a big occasion. In the afternoon quite a few of Claude's staff turned up and joined the party, and finally, when Caterina had fallen asleep from exhaustion, Katy carried her upstairs and put her to bed.

Katy sat by the little bed for a while, gently stroking the tumbled black curls from the small brow. She was a beautiful child; it seemed so unfair that she had lost her mother. With a deep sigh Katy stood up and, turning, walked out of the room, gently closing the door behind her. Very soon she herself would be a mother, and the enormity of her problem threatened to overwhelm her once again.

Determinedly she straightened her shoulders and descended the stairs. She was not going to think about her problems tonight. Claude's home was quickly filling up with his friends, quite a few of the models he used, and the adult party was getting underway.

Katy mingled with the guests, meeting old friends, listening to the gossip of the fashion world, the quite often bitchy comments, but more often funny ones. She danced and smiled and drank champagne, but as the clock passed midnight secretly she wished she could sneak off to her bedroom. But as Claude's hostess for the evening it wasn't possible.

It was after three when the final guest reluctantly departed, one of Claude's new models, a girl Katy had never seen before. She watched for a second the couple in a passionate clinch at the door, a wry smile curving her lips as she slowly made her way to the kitchen. Claude was incorrigible, she smiled softly to herself. A cup of coffee and bed was what she needed.

The coffee percolated, Katy poured herself a cup and sat down on the hard pine kitchen chair, propping her head up with one elbow on the table. She raised her eyes as the door swung open. 'So soon, Claude? Don't tell me you're losing your touch?' she joked.

'In deference to you, Katy, darling, I chased the girl off.' He helped himself to a cup of coffee and sat down opposite her. 'Jen is a very beautiful girl—lovely bone-structure, very photogenic—but unfortunately nothing between her ears, and any man between her legs.'

Katy choked on her coffee and burst out laughing. 'Claude, you are terrible!' she spluttered.

'I know, chérie, but at my age I am allowed to be. I am still a man and on occasions I need a woman. Once I almost tried for you. Until my son told me very firmly that as his wife's friend you were strictly out of bounds.'

Katy's head shot up, her eyes widening in surprise on Claude's attractive face, and what she saw in his eyes embarrassed her. He meant it...

'Don't worry, Katy,' he chuckled, reaching out to take her hand in his. 'Alain did not need to warn me off. I knew you were not for me. I stick to the Jens of this world; they know how the game is played, and no one gets hurt. You, on the other hand, are the serious-minded intelligent type who believes in love and marriage, hearth and home. My late wife was very like you.' His slender artistic fingers tightened slightly on hers. 'And for that reason I am going to break the rule of a lifetime and offer some advice.'

'Come off it, Claude, you're always giving advice.'

'About fashion, work, yes. But this is more personal.' Katy tensed and tried to ease her hand from his. 'Katy, I have known you for a long time, as an employee but more importantly as a friend of the family. I have watched you grow from a shy young girl to a beautiful sophisticated young woman, and I hate to see you hurting.'

'Whatever gave you that idea?' Katy tried to stop him. 'I love my new career... I'm doing well——'

'Katy, I read the papers. You and Jake Granton made the *Paris Match*. You forget how very popular you are in France. The caption read something like, "The lively Lena dragging the staid banker Granton into the limelight."'

'Oh, hell,' she muttered.

'I created the Lena image and I know it isn't you. You had to be dragged into going out. The rose garden you planted around the side of the house is still thriving. You were Anna's number-one babysitter. As for Granton, he has the money, but has never been one of the jet set, so I want to know what is going on. Something is not right somewhere.'

'Your imagination is working overtime, Claude,' Katy informed him coolly, but one look at his arched brow told her she was not going to get away with such a simple denial. 'I met Jake on the charity date, as you well know.' It still rankled that Claude had set her up for the mess she was now in.

'No, I didn't know. The publicity department of the charity arranged the date. I was under the impression it was the man at the show you were going out with.'

Katy's green eyes searched his face. He was telling the truth. 'That man was Jake's agent,' she said flatly. 'Anyway, one date led to another, and now I suppose you could say we're an item.'

'I gathered that much from the Press, and I was happy for you, until you arrived here yesterday. You will grant I have a lot more experience in affairs of the heart than you, and when I see a beautiful woman who has given up modelling, no longer needs to stay slim, has a new career she loves and is supposedly in love for the first time, common sense tells me you should have put on weight, not lost it. You looked like a wraith coming across that airport yesterday.'

'I still watch my figure,' she defended.

'Katy, I have rung your apartment every night for the past two weeks; at first it was to check if you were coming over for the party, and then my curiosity was aroused: you were never there. I am not going to pry any further. If you have moved in with the man, that is your business. But, Katy, don't fool yourself. Your sort of woman needs marriage.'

She pulled her hand free, and drained her now cold coffee. 'I know what I'm doing, Claude. You don't need to worry.'

'If you say so, Katy.' Claude stood up, and with a hand at her elbow helped her to her feet. 'But remember, Katy, if you need a friend or a home you will always be welcome here.'

'Thank you, Claude,' she whispered, emotion choking her. He was such a caring man, a true friend...

Katy fell asleep as soon as her head touched the pillow, and when two tiny fingers peeled back her eyelids, and she heard a voice shouting, 'Are you awake, Auntie Katy?' she groaned before leaping up and swinging Caterina over and into the bed.

She bid a tearful farewell to Claude, Alain and Caterina at the airport, and walked briskly to the waiting aircraft. She would be back in London in under an hour, and take a taxi to her father's in time for Sunday tea. There was no way Jake would ever know she had been abroad. In that she was wrong...

The cab drew to a halt outside her father's door. Katy opened her clutch-bag, found her purse, and with a muttered exclamation asked the taxi driver to wait. Stupidly she had not enough cash for the fare. She dashed up to the door and pressed the brass bell. 'Hurry up,' she murmured under her breath. The door swung open and quickly she stepped into the hall.

'Dad,' she shouted, 'I need some cab...' The words died in her throat as an all too familiar strong tanned hand gripped her arm and swung her around. She looked up into the furious face of Jake. What the hell was he doing here? She swallowed hard on the knot of fear clogging her throat and with an enormous effort of will she forced a smile to her lips. 'I need some cash for the taxi, Jake,' she demanded coolly.

His fingers bit into her arm and she winced in pain at the pressure. 'I will attend to the taxi, and then I will attend to you.' The threat was unmistakable. 'Say hello and goodbye to your father. We are leaving in a minute.'

She stood in the hall and watched his departing back, frozen in shock.

'Katy, dear. So you finally made it.' Her father's voice broke into her numb brain. 'Jake has been waiting ages for you, poor man.'

'Hello, Dad,' she mumbled, stunned at the collapse of her plan. Jake was supposed to be in Switzerland until Monday. 'I'm sorry——'

'Katy is sorry we can't stop, David,' Jake's sardonic voice interrupted. 'But we have a pressing appointment. I'm sure you understand, old man.'

Before Katy could gather her scattered wits she was being ushered out of the house.

'Just a minute!' she remonstrated as Jake, with his arm firmly around her waist, almost carried her along the pavement to where a smart black top of the range BMW was parked.

'Shut up and get in.'

A hand at her back shoved her none too gently into the passenger-seat. Her weekend case sailed over her head to land with a dull thud on the back seat. 'My God, that nearly hit me!' she exclaimed.

Jake slid into the driving seat and turned one hand on the steering-wheel, his other arm along the back of the seat. 'When I'm finished with you being hit by a suitcase will seem paltry in comparison, I promise you.' The sibilant rustle of his voice, the lowness of the tone, sent arrows of fear darting down her spine.

Katy raised her eyes to his and shrank back in the seat at the force of his rage. His black eyes gleamed like living coals of fire set in the harsh contours of his face. The skin pulled taut across his high cheekbones, a nerve twitched spasmodically in his tightly clenched jaw. Fury, inimical anger—there was no word to describe the hostility she could feel crashing over her like waves in a storm-tossed sea. She had never seen him so enraged.

'Don't you think you're over-reacting somewhat?' she offered quietly and, to her surprise, quite steadily. The car was moving and she felt emboldened to add, 'After all, Jake, we women are notorious for changing our minds.' Frantically she was searching for an excuse—anything to placate his anger.

'Shut up.' And she did. The rest of the ride was completed in absolute silence.

'Get out.'

Katy took one look at Jake's face and complied. He grabbed her arm and half dragged her into the lift. She tried to shake off his hand but he simply tightened his grip. As the lift rose her stomach sank, and the blood ran cold in her veins. Whatever excuse she came up with she had the horrible conviction Jake was not going to believe her, but then, did it matter? she asked herself. Their relationship had to end some time. Why not now?

Jake pushed her into the apartment and carefully locked the door after them, pocketing the key.

'Really, Jake, there's no need to be so melodramatic.' She tried to laugh. 'I stayed with some friends instead of Dad.' An instinct of self-preservation stopped her mentioning Paris.

'You lying little bitch.' Jake caught her shoulders and spun her around to face him. 'Your friend lives in Paris,' he snarled, his face only inches from her own.

'How——?'

'I paid the cab fare from Heathrow, my treacherous little Katy, and now you are going to pay me.' He tore the jacket from her shoulders and the blouse followed suit.

'No...' She struggled, but her effort was soon dashed as he swung her high and carried her into the bedroom, dropping her unceremoniously down on to the wide bed.

Jake towered over her, huge and terrifyingly menacing. Never had she seen him so consumed with anger. There was a barely controlled violence in the way he looked at her. She raised a hand to her throat in an involuntary gesture, betraying her fear.

'Yes, my darling Katy, I could throttle you with my bare hands, but first...' his eyes raked her crumpled form and with a minimum of effort he stripped the clothes from her body '...I am going to expunge the touch of your friend Claude from every pore of your body.'

'No, you've got it wrong!' she cried. 'Let me explain!' But she was too late.

Jake lowered his body on to the bed, trapping her slender body with his own. His mouth covered hers, insensitive to the pain he was causing as he savagely kissed her until she felt the taste of her own blood on her tongue. But the ravishment did not stop with a kiss.

His mouth searched and found the rosy tip of her breast while his hands roamed the length of her body with devastating thoroughness, teasing and tormenting until she whimpered in despair at her own frailty. Mindless, she wrapped her slender arms around him—she had no idea when he had shed his clothes—and her nails raked his broad back. She almost screamed as his mouth travelled lower to achieve her ultimate devastating capitulation. She heard her own voice begging him to take her.

Jake complied with one single savage thrust; her body arched off the bed and her long legs wrapped around his waist. Her keening cry was trapped in her throat as his mouth closed over hers again.

Later, how much later she had no idea, Jake rolled off the bed and stood looking down on her nakedness.

'You're a beautiful woman, Katy, but with the soul of a whore. I thought I could...' He stopped.

Katy flinched at the unadulterated hatred that shone in his dark eyes. 'Could what?' she whispered.

'Nothing. Pack your bags and get out. I never want to set eyes on you again.' And with that, totally unconscious of his own magnificent nudity, he casually picked up his clothes. He cast her one contemptuous glance and added, 'I want you out of here in half an hour. Anything you leave I will send on to your apartment,' and he walked out of the room.

She squeezed her eyes tightly closed. She would not cry. This was the end and perhaps it was for the best. At least she still had some pride. He would never know how much she loved him. Or that she was having his child. A harsh dry laugh rattled in her throat. The decision of whether to tell him about the baby was made for her. She had been frightened he would insist on marriage for the child's sake. When in reality if Jake knew he would probably insist on her getting rid of it. He would never tolerate a woman of her supposedly lax morals having his child . . .

CHAPTER NINE

KATY dragged herself up and swung her long legs over the side of the bed. She paused for a moment, her head bowed, her long golden hair falling like a tangled curtain either side of her face. Jake had told her to leave. It had had to happen some time, but like acid dropping on a stone the reality of her situation was seeping into her tired mind. The injustice of his remarks, his fury because she had gone to Paris and stayed with Claude, suddenly struck her as totally unfair.

So what if Jake did imagine Claude was her old lover? He never gave her a chance to explain; instead he had . . . She shuddered. The force of his lovemaking had totally swamped her feeble resistance, and her body had betrayed her yet again. She lifted her head, tossing the hair from eyes that were narrowed in fury. But not any more, she vowed silently.

She got to her feet and with quick, jerky movements she gathered underwear from the drawer and threw it on the bed. She selected a pair of briefs and a bra, and headed for the shower.

Five minutes later she returned to the bedroom, and, flinging open all the wardrobe doors, she methodically removed dresses, skirts, all her own clothes, and tossed them to join the rest on the bed. She took particular care not to include any of the garments Jake had tricked her into accepting on their visit to Venice.

With the hectic pace of their social life in the past few weeks she had been forced to wear some of the evening

159

clothes, as her own wardrobe was of excellent quality
but quite meagre.

She dragged the suitcases from the adjoining dressing-
room, cursing Jake under her breath. 'The swine, the
flaming hypocrite.' She stopped long enough to pull on
a pair of jeans and a soft blue lambswool sweater. Then,
picking up a hairbrush, she savagely brushed the tangles
from her hair and fastened it back in a pony-tail with a
pale blue silk scarf. She didn't care what she looked like.
She just wanted to get out.

Katy swept her arm along the dressing-table, emp-
tying the bottles and jars into the suitcase. She hesitated
at the small black lacquered jewellery box, her attention
caught by the glitter of diamonds. She picked out the
ring Jake had given her. A prop to fool an old lady.
Jake's devious idea. Like all his other ideas, the devil!

Her lips tightened in disgust, with herself as much as
him. She had allowed Jake to blackmail her into being
his mistress, and had actually nursed the hope that by
some miracle he might care for her, even though she knew
his motive was revenge.

She had actually been prepared to forget his original
reason for seducing her years ago. A smokescreen to de-
ceive her father while sleeping with his wife Monica.
God, but she had been a fool for far too long. A flash
of green, and the pendant he had given her for her eighteenth birthday went into the pocket of her jeans along
with the ring.

Well, Jake Granton was in for a big surprise, Katy
thought furiously. All the hurt and humiliation he had
inflicted on her bubbled to the surface and she physically shook with the force of her rage. She would leave
all right. Haphazardly she packed the first suitcase,
snapped it shut and dragged it to the door. The next
followed very quickly.

Katy was panting, her face red with her exertions and a fiercely burning anger. She marched down the hall and into the lounge, her green eyes shooting fire; for once in her life she was going to tell the arrogant, devious bastard just what she thought of him.

'Good, you're ready. I'll call a cab. Your apartment, or the airport and Claude?' Jake enquired silkily.

Katy looked at him. 'You supercilious swine!' She couldn't control her reaction. He was leaning negligently against the window-sill. Clad in a casual white sweat-shirt and hip-hugging black jeans, he looked wickedly attractive; a swift stab of regret pierced her anger, but she quickly stamped on her wayward feelings.

His autocratic profile tautened. 'I should have remembered the old adage, "One cannot make a silk purse out of a sow's ear." It was a mistake for me to try. Once a whore, always a whore,' he drawled insultingly and stepped away from the window.

His last insult was too much for Katy's fragile self-control. She dashed across the room and slapped her slender hand over his on the telephone.

'Not so fast!' she spat.

Jake glanced down at her hand against his; with his other hand he clasped her wrist between thumb and forefinger and lifted it away. His lips curved in a grimace of disdain and he dropped her hand as though it were a dead rat. 'I told you to get out; don't make me throw you out.'

The air crackled with barely contained animosity. She must have been mad to ever have imagined she loved him. Katy sizzled. She tilted her head to stare into black eyes as hard and expressionless as jet. He didn't need a mistress or a wife—a blown-up doll would have had enough emotion for him. Throw her out! she seethed. He wouldn't get the chance...

'Oh, I'm going, never fear, but first I am going to have the satisfaction of telling you exactly what I think of you. If I am a whore I am exactly what you made me,' she snarled. 'You barged back into my life and thought you could buy me for three thousand pounds. Jake Granton, the staid banker no publicity must touch. You even used an agent, though God knows what for— the date was very public. As for your bland assumption I would leap into bed with you, you conceited pig——'

'That's enough,' he cut in icily.

'No way—I'm only just starting.' Her small chin jutted belligerently. 'You blackmailer, I wonder what your City friends would think if they knew,' she sneered. 'You set me up simply because of dented male pride. Some tasteless revenge. You bought me, and I was stupid and cared enough about other people to let you. Something, Mr High and Mighty Granton, you deliberately used against me.'

Katy watched as his face darkened with suppressed anger. That got to him, she thought savagely, but she wasn't finished yet. 'Don't you think I guessed your little game the past few weeks? You made me into your mistress, and I, fool that I was, actually thought you might care for me.' In full flood, she didn't register the narrowing of Jake's eyes, or the flash of some unknown emotion flicker across his handsome face. 'Until you started dragging me around every nightclub and high-profile place in town. The use of my body wasn't enough for you. You had to publicly humiliate me.'

'No.'

She ignored his swift denial. 'You're a liar and a cheat without an honest bone in your body. You even lied to your own grandmother.' Katy shook her head. 'And you have the colossal nerve to quote asinine clichés at me.' She shoved her hands in the pockets of her jeans to try and stop them trembling, her fingers curled on something hard, and without a second thought she withdrew the ring and pendant from her pocket and flung them in Jake's face. 'Here—take back your props; I don't want them. Give them to the next woman you buy.'

Jake flinched as the jewellery scraped his face and fell to the floor. Slowly he bent down and retrieved the ring and pendant. He straightened and stared at the jewels in his hand for a long moment, then, catching Katy by the arm as she would have stormed off, he swung her around to face him. 'You kept this,' he rasped, the words apparently dragged out of him, the pendant dangling from his hand.

He could barely suffer to speak to her, he held her in such contempt, Katy thought raggedly, and suddenly she had to fight to retain her anger.

'Stupidly I thought it was a legitimate birthday present. Now I realise you gave it to me for services rendered that weekend.' The thought of the first time they had made love all those years ago brought a sudden rush of moisture to her eyes. She blinked; what a naïve idiot she had been, and it was all this man's fault.

'That is not true, Katy,' Jake said adamantly. 'It was a birthday present. I have never bought a woman in my life and I——'

Katy's harsh laugh echoed in the sudden silence of the room. 'No, Jake?' she queried cynically.

His dark brows drew together in a deep frown, his lips a tight line rimmed in white. He was fighting to retain his own temper. But Katy didn't care. He couldn't intimidate her; not any more.

'The truth hard to stomach, darling?' she jeered.

'I've listened to you rant and rave, but nothing alters the facts. You can blame me for some things. But Claude and all the others... I don't think so,' he said sardonically, his hand dropping from her shoulder as he turned and sank down on to the sofa. 'Get a cab and go, Katy.' He waved a dismissive hand in her direction, picked up a newspaper and began to read.

His casual dismissal was the last straw for Katy. Her slender control snapped completely, and with a fury she did not know she possessed she swiped the paper from his hands. 'All what others?' she cried. 'You sanctimonious bastard. There were no others. You saw to that. You spoilt me for any other man. I gave you everything, believed your protestations of love, only to find out the truth about you just in time.'

Katy was not aware of Jake sitting up straighter on the sofa, the fierce tension tautening his large frame. Her eyes were fixed on his face but she did not really see him; she was reliving his first bitter betrayal.

'What truth, Katy?' The urgency in his tone escaped her; all she heard was the trace of cynicism.

She laughed, a harsh jangling sound, on the edge of hysteria. 'Monica! What about Monica, Jake?' she raged. 'My once stepmother, the lady you told me to try and get along with. Remember that, Jake? The lady you were bedding on a regular basis beneath her husband's, my father's, very nose.'

Katy, her emotions running riot, shot him a fulminating look of sheer hatred. 'I didn't go to France because I wanted to broaden my horizons; I went because I couldn't stomach the way you had used me, or intended to go on using me, even to offering marriage to hide your miserable affair.'

Suddenly Katy felt sick: she had told him more than she had ever wanted him to know. She swung around on one heel, stalked across the room and picked up a suitcase. Her rage was extinguished like a spent firework on the fourth of July.

Why bother? she asked herself. The man was without conscience or morals and his integrity was on a par with Attila the Hun. She was only hurting herself dredging up the past. She had to get away before she was physically sick.

She reached the door and her hand grasped the lock to open it. Jake had said not a word. But then why would he? she thought bitterly; he could not deny her charges. He was a low-down skunk of a man, and she had wasted quite enough of her life loving him. She breathed deeply and turned the key. From now on she was going to be her own woman. She had a good career in front of her, a child of her own to look forward to. Who needed a man? she asked herself.

She pushed open the door, but something held her back; she turned, unable to resist one last look at the man she had loved so deeply and for so long.

Jake was sitting where she had left him, his dark head thrown back, his face grey beneath his tan, his eyes tightly closed, his sensuous lips pressed together as though he were in pain. He looked as though someone had punched him in the stomach.

Katy hesitated; she had never seen him like this. Was he ill? 'Jake.' She whispered his name, although her common sense told her to leave.

His eyes opened, his dark gaze trapped hers, and she was incapable of breaking the contact. He looked as she expected a wounded stag must feel as the hunter's unseen bullet pierced its heart. Uncertainty, sorrow and pain mingled in the brown depths of Jake's thickly lashed eyes. He looked vulnerable as she had never imagined he could.

She took a step towards him, but abruptly drew back as he leapt to his feet, his face contorting into a mask of demonic rage. Vulnerable, Jake? She must be going weak in the head...Katy turned to leave.

A hand on her arm swung her around. Jake, dark eyes flashing fire, pinned her back against the wall, his lower torso thrust against her flat stomach. Katy lashed out at him with both hands, but with insulting ease he caught them and spread her arms wide either side of her head, his strong hands like manacles around her fine-boned wrists.

For a fleeting instant she feared for her life, he was so enraged. And she had mistakenly thought he looked ill, uncertain. What a joke! She saw his mouth working, but no sound came out. 'I—I'm going...' She had delayed too long in leaving. Was he now going to bodily throw her out?

'Shut up, you stupid little bitch.'

She quailed before the force of his anger, and her breast heaved against the soft wool of her sweater; fear and, to her shame, the touch of his muscular thighs, hard against her, were arousing other basic emotions.

'Monica! You dare accuse me of sleeping with your stepmother? Are you mad, woman?'

'No, but you obviously are,' Katy responded, slightly breathless. 'What's the matter, Jake, can't you stomach the fact I've always known about Monica? Makes your high moral garbage about Claude sound pretty stupid,' she said mockingly.

'I have never slept with Monica in my life, not before she married your father, when she was married, or since. If you have dared to suggest such a thing to David or anyone else I will wring your pretty neck.' His brown eyes burnt black with the intensity of his rage. 'When I think of the years I have wasted, and all because you in your childish imagining walked out on me. I could kill you. But not before I make love to you until you're senseless. How could you do that to us?' he demanded with a shake of his dark head, as though the idea was beyond his comprehension. 'How could you think I would stoop so low?'

'How could I?' she screeched. He was a great actor, but she didn't believe one word of his explosive denial. It was far too late in coming. 'I could, Jake, because I saw you with my own eyes. There's no point in your vehement denials. I might have been young but I was never stupid, except where you were concerned. I honestly believed you visited our house to see me. Until the last time when I was eighteen and left school.'

'Explain,' Jake prompted, his body moving restlessly against her.

Katy recognised the signs: his anger was abating, but the black gleam in his brown eyes was no less fierce. Her gaze slid to his mouth, his warm breath caressed her forehead, and she knew if she did not get away fast she would not be able to resist the subtle changes in his body language.

'Let go of my arms,' she requested. 'I can't think when you're towering over me like some great dinosaur.' And, to her surprise, he did.

She took a deep breath to ease the tension. She felt his glance slide to where her breasts pushed taut against the fabric of her sweater, but refused to be intimidated by the knowing smile that quirked his sensuous lips.

'Is that better?' he demanded softly.

It wasn't; although they were no longer touching, his strong hands rested against the wall either side of her head, effectively imprisoning her. His anger had definitely abated, but she had a sneaking suspicion a soft-voiced Jake was a lot more dangerous. She rubbed her hands down her jeans-clad hips in a nervous gesture.

'Get on with it, Katy, and your explanation had better be good or I might still do you an injury,' he threatened.

Katy wished she had kept her mouth shut, but, meeting and holding his gaze, she registered the speculative, almost eager gleam in his eyes, and somehow it gave her confidence.

Quickly she explained her return a day early and what she had seen and heard. As she spoke Jake tensed, then stood up straight, his hands falling by his sides.

'All this time... four years you have carried that opinion of me round in your head, because of a conversation you overheard. Our years of friendship you honestly thought were all a lie on my part. An excuse to bed your stepmother. Have I got that right?' he demanded hardily.

'Yes.'

His rapier-like glance raked from her head to toe as though he had never seen her before. 'And of course it never once occurred to you to ask me for an explanation?' he demanded derisively.

'No. Why should I?' she said bluntly, and with a defiant toss of her head she gave it to him straight. 'I heard Monica remind you of your wonderful weekend together when you went skiing and never left the hotel. You were in each other's arms. I might have been young and naïve, but there was nothing wrong with my hearing or my eyesight,' she concluded sarcastically.

With a shrug Jake turned and strode across the room. She watched him warily for a moment. There was a defeated look to the stoop of his wide shoulders. He ran a hand distractedly through his black hair, and while his back was turned Katy took a hesitant step towards the still open door, but she must have made some sound because Jake spun round.

'Wait, Katy. I think I can explain.'

'Don't bother,' she muttered mutinously and bent to pick up her suitcase.

'Please, Katy, don't go. Hear me out; surely you owe me that much?'

She stopped, and, straightening up, lifted her head. Jake had moved and was once more standing in front of her, but this time he made no attempt to touch her. She raised suspicious green eyes to his. What was he playing at? Five minutes ago he was threatening to throw her out; now he was actually pleading with her to stay.

She hardened her heart. 'I don't owe you a thing, buster; as far as I'm concerned you have been paid in full,' she stated firmly.

'Please listen,' he demanded urgently. 'I remember that night well. How could I forget it? That was the night I formally asked David for your hand in marriage. We had dined together and naturally Monica was there. Afterwards Monica and I had some business to discuss and your father went to bed.'

'Some business!' Katy snorted derisively.

'I don't know why Monica behaved as she did; perhaps she heard you arrive and wanted to stir up trouble. I've known her a long time, and she has a very twisted sense of humour. I was stunned when she threw her arms around me and started talking about *us*. I quickly disentangled myself and left about five minutes later.'

'Hmph!' Katy snorted. 'And I suppose next you will tell me you never went on holiday with her.'

'I am telling you the truth, Katy. As for the skiing weekend, Monica came on one of our regular trips to Switzerland—not as my companion, but with a friend of mine from college. When she said we never left the hotel it was because I had broken my leg and she had broken her ankle. I can understand how it must have sounded to you, but it was entirely innocent.'

Katy looked searchingly at his darkly handsome face. Innocent, he said. She doubted if Jake had had an innocent relationship with a woman other than his mother the whole of his life. He was far too virile, much too much a man, and she would have to be fifty kinds of idiot to believe a word he said. Anyway, it was no longer relevant. He had spent the past weeks dragging her all over town, so her dismissal from his life would be very public, and all for some petty vengeance.

'Well, thanks for the explanation, but it was a lifetime ago, Jake. Right now would you mind calling me a taxi, and I'll get out of here?'

'You don't believe me, do you?' He shook his dark head. 'You don't want to believe me...'

'It's not necessary that I believe you——'

'What the hell would you know what is necessary, with your rigid little mind?' he cut her off sarcastically, and, picking up her other case, he added, 'There is no need for a cab. I'll drive you—it will be quicker.'

Katy did not deign to argue. He was in a hurry to get rid of her, she thought bleakly. So much for his pat explanation! In a very short while he would be out of her life for good. All the arguments and recriminations in the world could not change that fact. Silently she followed him to the car.

They had been travelling for some time, when Katy realised Jake was not taking her to her apartment, and as she looked out of the window, and saw the sign for Heathrow Airport fade away, obviously Paris was not on the agenda either.

'Where are we going?' she blurted. Jake shot her a sidelong glance, his lips twisted in an ironic smile.

'I wondered how long it would take you to break your sullen silence and acknowledge me,' he drawled mockingly.

Acknowledge him? Didn't he realise she was aware of every movement of his lithe body, the muscles rippling in his thighs as his feet operated the pedals, his long fingers lightly clasping the steering-wheel with supreme confidence? It was a constant battle for her to mask just how very much aware of him she was.

'This is not the way to my apartment and we have passed the airport,' she said firmly. 'I want to——'

'What you want, Katy, is the truth, and if you can bring yourself to humour me for a few hours that is exactly what you're going to get. Now shut up and go to sleep. You look shattered and it will be a while before we arrive at our destination.'

'Adding kidnapping to blackmail, are we?' she drawled, but her words lacked force. The anger that had kept her going for the past couple of hours had seeped away. Katy could feel the pain growing inside her and her eyes ached with unshed tears. Why Jake was prolonging her agony she had no idea. Maybe it was male pride; he refused to let her have the last word. Yet his attempts at justification for his actions were so pathetic as to be laughable.

He glanced across at her, one dark brow arched sardonically. 'Sarcasm does not become you, sweetheart. Do as you're told. Trust me, for once in your life.'

She looked at his hard profile; his attention was once again fixed on the road in front. His earlier anger and the uncertainty she had sensed before was gone. He was all virile, confident male. Trust him, he said! She would as soon trust a rattlesnake. She opened her mouth to demand he take her home, and closed it again.

Inconsequentially she remembered a popular quote in France. The great Maurice Chevalier once said, 'Many a man has fallen in love with a girl in a light so dim he would not have chosen a suit by it.' The same was true for women, she thought sadly. She loved Jake, and yet there was no good reason for her passion.

Jake had seduced her at eighteen and betrayed her. Blackmailed her at twenty-two. Now he seemed intent on abducting her. Love was certainly blind in her case. If she had any common sense at all she should have had him arrested by now. Instead she sank back in her seat, and closed her eyes, praying her ordeal would soon be over, and she could walk away from him with some remnant of her pride intact.

CHAPTER TEN

A HAND on her shoulder woke her from a deep sleep. Katy blinked and opened her eyes. It was dark outside, the glare of the car headlights the only illumination in the black velvet of the night.

Slowly she sat up, blushing as she realised she had been asleep with her head on Jake's shoulder. 'Where are we?' she demanded, smoothing a few loose tendrils of hair back over her head, and pulling her sweater neatly down over her waist.

'You will soon see,' was Jake's enigmatic reply as he got out of the car.

She watched him for a second, but her gaze was distracted as a full moon appeared from behind the clouds, bathing the landscape in a wash of silver. She noted the rolling lawns running down to stop at a band of black leafless skeletal trees outlined against the night sky, and through a small gap a headland, and moonlight on water—the sea. She swung round in the seat, and in a daze stepped out of the car. The place was achingly familiar, but it couldn't be, she told herself.

Katy breathed deeply, filling her lungs with the cool salt-scented night air. Her green eyes, wide as saucers, roamed over the massive granite structure before her. Elegant stone steps led to a large double oak door that swung open as she watched, sending out a beam of golden light. She raised her head: over the door a beautiful arched stained-glass window sent a kaleidoscope of colours flickering across the car.

Katy gasped, and took a step forward. It was her old home. The outline of a miner in coloured glass confirmed it. 'Jake, wait!' she cried, running up the steps after him. She grabbed his arm. 'You can't barge in here. My father sold it.'

'Don't panic, Katy; we are expected.' He took her hand in his and tugged it under his arm, forcing her to accompany him into the house.

She cast a frantic glance at the elderly man standing in the entrance hall, and mumbled, 'Good evening.' What was Jake doing? she thought furiously. Was the place a hotel now? God knew, it was big enough. She had a vivid memory of herself as a child, and only having just learned to count, going methodically round the house counting every room and cupboard, the grand total thirty-five.

She blinked back her tears; the hall was just as she remembered, the floor highly polished stripped oak, the elegant staircase with the lovely banister she had slid down many a time in the past. She squeezed her eyes shut as the memories swamped her mind.

In a state of shock, she allowed Jake to lead her into the dining-room, and she sat on the chair he held out for her without a murmur. Even the furniture was the same. The large polished oak dining-table gleamed in the subdued lighting. Obviously it was not a hotel. Greedily she looked around, filling her senses with the house she had always adored. But as she slowly got over the shock of being there so unexpectedly Katy began to notice subtle differences. Whoever owned her old home now had certainly spent a lot of money on it.

A new Chinese silk carpet covered the polished floor; the walls were papered in what looked like a Sanderson silk in rich shades of blue and gold; the drapes at the long windows were also new, the deep Austrian blinds ruffled and trimmed in toning colours adding to the air of old elegance.

Katy's glance finally settled on the man seated opposite her. 'Jake,' she demanded urgently, 'how did we get here? How did they know we were coming?' She didn't understand what was going on. They had left the apartment in London, supposedly to part for good. Jake's throaty laugh burst into her troubled thoughts. 'It isn't funny.'

'To answer your question, a car telephone; but food first, Katy, and then we will talk, hmm...?'

The dining-room door opened and any reply Katy might have made was stopped in her throat. The elderly gentleman in typical butler's garb entered, pushing a trolley loaded with silver dishes. She glanced down at her worn jeans and old sweater. She should have changed for dinner. The occupants of the house would not be impressed by her rather too casual attire. 'Jake, I must get changed. What——?'

'Relax, Katy, and enjoy your food; there won't be anyone else joining us, I can assure you.'

How did he walk into her mind like that? she wondered for the thousandth time. Then for the next half-hour Katy munched her way through iced melon, followed by a delicious fresh salmon steak in a thick creamy sauce, and a massive slice of chocolate fudge cake with fresh cream, and to Katy it all tasted like sawdust. When the old man arrived with the cheese and biscuits she was ready to knock Jake's head off.

All through the meal he had flatly refused to answer any of her questions. If he said 'later' one more time she would kick him. She was bursting with curiosity and Jake was smiling like the cat that caught the canary but refusing to enlighten her.

'Come along, Katy; I can see the suspense is killing you.' Rising, he walked around the table and helped her to her feet.

'What the hell is going on?' she demanded.

Jake smiled down into her flushed face, his dark eyes gleaming. 'Patience.' And, flinging an arm casually around her shoulder, he ushered her out into the hall and across into what she remembered as the drawing-room.

She should have shaken off his arm, she told herself, but was reluctant to part with the comfort he offered. Her mind was in a spin and her legs felt none too steady. Meekly she allowed him to pull her down beside him on a large over-stuffed sofa, her eyes darting around the room in wonder and delight.

This room, she recalled, had been very formal with stiff high-backed leather chairs, and hard leather chesterfields. Now it was a symphony in pinks and greens, with matching fabrics and drapes, the ceiling a dreamy pink with the deep cornices and mouldings picked out in a rosy white. From the picture rail hung a delightful collection of water-colours, all depicting the Cornish countryside. Over the elegant marble fireplace a larger portrait of a young girl had pride of place.

Katy's mouth fell open in shock. It was herself at thirteen. She remembered her father insisting she have her portrait painted as a birthday present for him. When she had thought about it at all she had assumed her father still owned it.

'Now are you beginning to understand?' Jake's voice asked softly in her ear.

She jumped at the intrusion into her troubled thoughts. 'No, I am not,' she responded flatly, and, turning wary eyes to his, she searched his face for some glimmer of enlightenment.

Jake took her two hands in his and held them on his thigh, his dark head bent to mask his expression from her. 'The house is mine, Katy.'

Jake's! She couldn't believe it. Katy made to pull her hands free, but his fingers only clasped her small hands tighter. Sitting so close to him, his shoulder brushing hers, their knees touching, was having an unsettling effect on her overwrought nerves.

'Do you remember when and why your father sold it?' he asked in an oddly unsure tone.

'How could I forget?' she said bitterly. It still hurt even now. 'Darling Monica hated the country, had no intention of being stuck in the middle of Cornwall for the rest of her life. I can't see why you need to ask, Jake; if you remember you were there at the time. I was fifteen and you told me I should accept my father's wishes, and everything would be OK. Another lie!' She snorted inelegantly.

'Exactly, Katy: you were fifteen, I had known you for one year, and I bought this house from your father. Think about it. If, as you imagined, I was having a red-hot affair with Monica why would I spend a fortune on a house she hated?'

She stared at Jake dumbly, unable to speak. His dark brown eyes watched her with a strange intensity as if he was willing her to reach some conclusion. She frowned. 'I did wonder if your flat in town was your only home.' She spoke her thoughts out loud. 'It is nice, but with your wealth——'

'I sold my boyhood home when Father died and kept this one; surely that tells you something?'

What was he trying to say? Katy puzzled. He had bought her old home, certainly not for Monica. He fancied it, she thought, and with a shrug of her shoulders she told him so.

'True, I like the house, but as I'm a bachelor it's far too large for me. I bought it with one particular person in mind.'

'One particular person,' she parroted.

'Yes.' His lips curved in a lazy smile and quite deliberately he raised his eyes to the portrait over the mantelpiece.

Deep down inside a tiny flicker of hope unfurled. Was Jake trying to say he'd bought it for her? Could it be possible...? Could she have been wrong about him and Monica? A snippet of conversation popped unheralded into her head. He had told her last week he had broken his leg not once but twice while skiing. His story about the hotel could be true...

'You broke your leg twice.' She had not meant to say it out loud.

'Yes, Katy.' His dark eyes returned to her flushed face, his strong tanned hands gently lifted hers to his lips, and in a curiously reverent gesture he pressed a kiss to each palm.

'Now do you understand?' he queried smoothly.

Katy had spent too long mistrusting him, hating him, to immediately believe him. Her sea-green eyes, wide and wary, searched his handsome features, looking for some sign that would convince her. If she believed he had bought the house for her, then that meant...his marriage proposal and everything had been genuine... She wanted to believe him, oh, how she wanted to, but he had hurt her too much...

Jake sighed and dropped her hands. 'You aren't going to make this easy for me.' He stood up and walked across to the mantelpiece, his back towards her. 'But then, why should you? I've treated you abominably, and I have no excuse. Jealousy is an unenviable emotion, and can be no justification for the way I've behaved.'

'Jealousy,' she parroted again. Jake jealous of her... somehow the thought made the flicker of hope in her heart burn a little brighter. He turned around, leaning one elbow on the mantelpiece in apparent ease, but she noted his brown eyes flickered over her and fixed on some point on the opposite wall, almost as though he was afraid to look at her.

'Hard to believe, Katy? Well, I can assure you it is true. But perhaps I should start at the beginning. Do you want a drink? Because I certainly do.'

His quick change of subject threw Katy, and she mumbled a refusal and waited with building impatience as he strode to the drinks cabinet and, picking up a bottle, poured a very large whisky into a crystal tumbler. Her fascinated gaze watched the muscles of his strong throat as he gulped most of it down at one go. 'The beginning,' she reminded him softly.

Jake still refused to look at her; instead his gaze was fixed on the portrait. 'I bought the painting along with the house, though David took some persuading to part with it. It is a very good likeness. It reminded me of the first day we met. I waited in the headmistress's study, expecting to have to tell a young schoolgirl the sad news of her mother's death, and escort her to her home. I only agreed to do it because I had promised my grandmother to look up your family and make sure Meldenton was all right. Latins take a debt of honour very seriously.'

Jake half smiled. 'Anyway, when you walked into the room I felt as though I had been kicked in the stomach. You had just come from the tennis court. Your glorious hair was floating like a cloud of gold almost down to your waist. You were wearing a white knit sports shirt, and a tiny pleated skirt that barely covered your behind, and your legs...'

Katy leaned forward on the sofa the better to hear. Jake was talking so low—virtually to himself. He must have heard her move, as he turned and gave her a wry smile.

'You were fully developed at fourteen and I had never seen anyone as beautiful in my life. Even now I don't know how I managed to keep my hands off you. I could not believe what had happened to me. I was a mature adult male, a staid banker, and I had the hots for a schoolgirl. I tried to hide it, and I tried to comfort and support you until after the funeral, but it was agony for me. I felt so damned guilty.'

'Guilty? But you were the model of decorum.' Katy grinned; suddenly her heart felt lighter, and the flame of hope burnt even brighter.

'Only because for the next twelve months I stayed away from you.'

'The postcards,' she murmured; he had kept in touch.

'Yes. God, I felt as guilty as hell, but I couldn't break all contact.' He paused. 'I kept thinking, this can't be happening to me, obsessed by a schoolgirl. It was my grandmother who made me see sense. I confessed my feelings to her, and she laughed; she reminded me I was half-Italian, and convinced me. For an Italian the age-gap between you and me would seem unimportant in a few years. So I began to pay more attention to Meldenton and I became a friend of your father, but my real motive was always to be with you.'

Katy stared at him, wide-eyed. Was this the man who had been telling her to get out of his life just hours earlier?

'All of which proves, from the moment I met you,' a slightly shamed smile twisted his lips, 'I was fascinated, intrigued, besotted with you. To be honest I was also thoroughly ashamed and, looking back, I can see it was my own guilt that got in the way of our relationship.'

Katy tried to speak, but Jake crossed the room and, catching her hands, pulled her to her feet. His hands stroked up to her shoulders, and held her firmly only inches away from his hard, tense body.

'But Monica was never an issue between you and me. That much you have to believe, Katy.'

'You told me to try and get along——' He stopped her.

'Only because I wanted to protect you, look after you, and I thought it better that your father was married, rather than running free.'

'Chasing everything in skirts,' Katy supplied for him with an ironic smile.

'Anyway, that is the only reason I advised you to try and get on with your stepmother. God knows, I hardly knew Monica; our bank had always handled her family's business, but she was an acquaintance... no more, I swear.'

The wheels of Katy's mind spun furiously. 'Your bank still handles her business.'

'Yes, unfortunately, but that will change when I go back to town, I promise.'

So that was how Jake had been able to vote Monica's shares at the board meeting, Katy thought. But remembering the board meeting brought Jake's blackmailing to her mind. She could not put her thoughts into words. She was too confused.

Jake waited for a while, absently fiddling with the scarf holding back her hair, until accidentally it came free, and with a gentle gesture he smoothed her heavy golden locks down over her shoulders. Then he looked straight into her eyes and said seriously, 'Katy, I have never loved any woman in my life the way I love you. You have to believe me. I bought this house from your father for you, sure that one day it would be our home.'

Katy's mouth trembled and she tried to speak, but once again the words would not come. He had said he loved her. As for Monica, she believed his explanation—well, most of it, she qualified silently. The picture in her mind of Jake with his arms around that woman still rankled. But if there was to be any hope of a relationship between Jake and herself she was going to have to take some things on trust. 'I believe you——' She was about to continue cautiously 'about the house', but Jake never gave her the chance.

'Katy! God, Katy!' He hauled her hard against him, his arms wrapped around her so tight that she could feel the heavy beating of his heart against her own. Then his mouth covered hers. He kissed her with a wild savage hunger that lit an answering response in Katy.

Somehow they were on the sofa, Jake's long body over hers; his hands were at her sweater, and he would have pulled it off, when suddenly he stopped.

'No, Katy...' Jake breathed unsteadily. He rolled to one side and curved his arms firmly around her so they were lying side by side. Gently he brushed back a lock of unruly hair from her brow, and stared at her, the banked-down passion in his black eyes fiercely controlled.

'Why, Jake?' She did not understand what had stopped him.

'Because, my love, for weeks we have made love, and instead of resolving our differences it has driven us further apart. In my conceit I thought, once I got you in my bed and made love to you again, you would forget about any other men and soon learn to love me. Now I see I was totally wrong.'

'Not totally wrong...' Katy murmured; she was not quite prepared to admit she loved him, but she couldn't let him think she didn't care. Jake's dark eyes flared with...was it hope?

'Ah, Katy, you can't imagine how good it makes me feel to hear you say that. This afternoon I thought I had blown my last chance with you.'

'You told me to get out,' she reminded him.

'My unreasonable jealousy,' he confessed. 'The odd thing is, when you first left me to go to Paris I was hurt, angry, but not jealous. I think I accepted your excuse that you wanted to see the world so easily because in my heart of hearts I knew I had rushed you into an adult relationship, and felt terribly guilty. I told myself I had to give you time to grow up, go to college, and when I received your letter saying you had met a young man I was hurt and madly jealous, but consoled myself with the fact that you were very young, and as long as I hung in there, kept in touch, eventually I would get you back. I carried on sending you cards, flowers, praying you wouldn't forget me.'

Katy smiled; it had puzzled her why he had bothered.

'When I saw the first pictures of you modelling, and the rumours in the Press about you, I was angry, but oddly pleased; obviously the young man had not lasted. I decided it was time I went to Paris and renewed my claim on you. Two years was long enough, and if the gossip was true you had had quite enough of a fling. It was time I married you. When I met you with Anna and her husband and saw how you behaved with Claude I was livid.' His arms tightened around her. 'I had worried about the age-difference between us, and there you were with a man old enough to be your father. I called you some terrible names.'

Katy shivered slightly as she remembered that particular meeting. It was the first time she had seen Jake really angry. 'Anna had just married Alain, Claude's son, and there was never anything between Claude and me,' she explained. 'I behaved the way I did because I did not want to admit I knew about Monica.'

'There was nothing to know about Monica.' Jake shook his head ruefully. 'And I'm beginning to realise I have been a complete fool about Claude. Anna's father-in-law, you say?'

'Yes.' In a rush of words she told him about Claude and her god-daughter Caterina. Suddenly it seemed very important to Katy that he should know the truth.

'Oh, God, Katy, can you ever forgive me?' Jake groaned. 'When I think what I've said and done in the past few weeks I cringe; my only excuse is I didn't know if I was on my head or my heels with you. You were marvellous in my bed but so uncaring the rest of the time, and I intended everything to be so different.'

'What exactly did you intend?' Katy asked softly. 'I could never understand why a man like you, who dislikes publicity, would pay so much money to take me out on a charity date.'

Jake chuckled, his dark eyes lit with laughter. 'You're never going to believe me, but I owe you the truth. I decided after four celibate years without you to make one last attempt to capture you. I thought long and hard about our previous relationship, and I realised, although we had spent a lot of time together, it was always at your home. I very rarely took you out. I think it was because you were so young, and in a way I was ashamed of my feelings for you. I reached the conclusion that I had deprived you of a proper courtship.'

'A courtship!' she exclaimed with a smile. 'What a very old-fashioned word, and a bit late, considering you had already had your evil way with me,' she joked while her mind registered 'celibate'.

'Do you want to hear this or not?' Jake demanded hardily, but the quirk of his lips belied his serious tone.

'Yes, please.' She snuggled closer and allowed her hand to stroke teasingly over his hip and thigh. 'But will it take much longer?' The flicker of hope had exploded in to a full-blown flame. Jake had freely admitted there had been no one else for him in all the years they had been apart, and instinctively she believed him.

'Anyway, I decided to wine and dine you, but first I had to persuade you to go out with me. The charity date was like a gift from heaven. I told myself I did not care about your other men or whether the stories in the Press about you were true. I could control my jealousy. I was your first lover and I was determined to be your last . . . But I blew it on our date.' He tapped the end of Katy's nose with an admonishing finger. 'And you, my dear Katy, didn't help. You let me think the worst of you—even encouraged me, too.'

'It was my defence,' she whispered. 'Otherwise we would have made love and it would have confirmed your low opinion of me.'

Jake's finger dropped to her lips and gently outlined the contours of her mouth. 'Are you confessing you wanted me, Katy?' he asked throatily.

'What do you think?' She captured his finger between pearly teeth and bit it. 'Why else would I agree to your dishonourable proposal to be your mistress? The family firm is important to me, but anyone but you and I would never have accepted. You were my first and only lover,' she confessed.

'Only lover. . .' he repeated wonderingly, reading the truth in her huge green eyes, and for a long moment silence reigned as their lips met and clung. Jake's large muscular body stirred restlessly against her, igniting the flames of passion with every movement.

'I'm sorry, Katy, so sorry,' he rasped against her mouth, and, putting some space between them, continued, 'I never intended to make you my mistress.' His black eyes burnt into hers, intent and oddly vulnerable. 'I would never have asked that of you, Katy. I admit I planned to coerce you into my life, but I wanted to marry you. If you remember that day in the boardroom, you never gave me the chance. You got in first, telling me you would rather die than marry me.'

Katy remembered, and her own embarrassment at the time when she'd thought she had jumped to the wrong conclusion, and Jake had laughed at her. 'You laughed,' she prompted.

'I laughed to hide my hurt, and on the spur of the moment decided to make you my mistress. I was so desperate and, I confess, furious with you that I didn't care how I got you as long as I succeeded. The trip to Venice was a stroke of genius on my part, I thought. It meant I got you to wear my ring, buy the trousseau and attend the engagement party. By the time we returned to London I was convinced the wedding was a certainty.' He tilted her chin with one hand and added accusingly, 'Until you took off my ring.'

Katy blinked at the fierce expression on his handsome face, but she was not intimidated. Her heart sang. Jake had wanted to marry her. She beamed; a smile of pure joy lighting her lovely face. 'You mean the second-hand ring for the second-hand woman?' she teased, but with a serious edge. His words had cut her to the quick at the time.

'God, Katy, I'm sorry. On our journey to Venice you looked so beautiful; the girl I'd loved as a child had turned into an elegant, sophisticated woman. I had made love to you the night before, but I was no nearer knowing the woman you had become. I was nervous, unsure, and naïvely I imagined that once I got my ring on your finger my troubles would be over, until you started to say you didn't want it.'

'I hated the thought of wearing a ring to fool your friends, to maintain your impeccable reputation,' she confessed. 'Now if it had been genuine...!' she grinned.

Jake frowned. 'The ring belonged to Grandmother Granton, and has always been passed down the female side of the family.' His serious explanation made Katy smile even wider. 'I would never have insulted you with anything but the genuine article, Katy.' Then slowly, reading the message in her gorgeous green eyes, he began to smile, a triumphant all-masculine grin. 'If I put the ring on your finger now, would you keep it?' he demanded hardily. 'And the commitment the ring implies?'

He was once again the arrogant man she knew and loved, all trace of vulnerability gone. But she still had a couple of queries before confessing her love completely. 'Why were you back from Switzerland so fast?'

'Because, my darling girl, one night away from you and I missed you like hell.' Their lips met in a very satisfying kiss.

'Oh, Jake, you really are a romantic at heart.' She smiled into his dark eyes and was rewarded with such a look of love and longing that her heart turned over in her breast.

'Damn it, I may as well confess all. My plan to court you had worked too well. There was a French reporter at the hotel who recognised me. He had the audacity to suggest, because you were not with me, that our affair was over. I felt like punching him on the jaw. Instead I told him that, on the contrary, you and I were to be married, and I hotfooted it back to England in case anyone else got the wrong idea.'

Katy silently blessed the French reporter.

'You still haven't answered my question,' Jake reminded her sombrely, and with just the slightest hint of vulnerability.

Katy could not resist teasing him. 'I will when you answer mine. Why did you drag me to every night-spot in London?'

'For the same reason I bought that bloody showy white Roller,' he responded impatiently. 'I told you before: I was attempting to "court" you, for want of a better word. On our charity date you said I had never taken you out, and certainly not in a white Rolls, and I thought it was what you wanted.'

It was Katy's turn to laugh, and in seconds Jake was joining in.

'God, Katy, it's a beautiful car, but I felt such a pretentious twit driving it. I have never been so relieved as when you said you did not like it and I could get back to my black BMW.'

'It won't be completely wasted, Jake. I can ride to our wedding in it.'

'Did you . . . will you . . . does that mean . . . ?'

'Yes, Jake.' She pressed her lips to his in a kiss full of love and laughter. 'Just one last thing: I love you and I love this house, but——'

He pulled her closer, moulding her to his hard form. 'No buts, Katy; not any more.'

'I wondered about your work. Fowey is hardly convenient for you, Jake.'

Jake jumped up and, catching her hand, he pulled her to her feet. 'A guided tour is in order—one that ends in the bedroom, my love.'

Half an hour later Katy stood in the master bedroom, breathless, her green eyes luminous with love as she stared into Jake's handsome grinning face. He looked ten years younger and inordinately pleased with himself as he slipped the emerald and diamond ring on her finger.

'Satisfied, Katy, darling? I don't think I have missed anything. Do you?'

The house was a revelation, beautifully modernised but retaining all the original features. Except for the west wing, where to her amazement Jake had installed a mainframe computer and a suite of offices for himself, and a magnificent studio for Katy. It must have taken him months, if not years; the proof of his love was all around her.

'Oh, Jake,' she whispered, 'I do love you,' her eyes swimming with tears of happiness.

His fingers brushed her lips. 'Keep saying that, Katy, for the rest of our lives. I want you, I need you, I love you, and I will never let you out of my sight again... We are getting married as soon as is humanly possible, and no more argument.'

'Yes, Jake.' His lips replaced his fingers as he swung her up in his arms and gently laid her down on the wide bed.

'Now we have everything,' he breathed triumphantly as he lowered his hard male body down beside her, and gathered her once more into his arms.

Katy moved her hands and slipped them under his sweater, felt the warmth of his firm flesh beneath her fingertips, and she hugged him with all her might. Jake nuzzled her throat, and a deep sigh of pure contentment escaped her. At last secure in her love for him, she could not resist teasing him.

'Not quite, Jake.'

Jake lifted his head, his black eyes puzzled. 'What else?'

'You forgot the nursery.' For once Katy had the last word...

HARLEQUIN PRESENTS®

A Year
DOWN UNDER

In 1993, Harlequin Presents celebrates the land down under. In June, let us take you to the Australian Outback, in OUTBACK MAN by Miranda Lee, Harlequin Presents #1562.

Surviving a plane crash in the Australian Outback is surely enough trauma to endure. So why does Adrianna have to be rescued by Bryce McLean, a man so gorgeous that he turns all her cherished beliefs upside-down? But the desert proves to be an intimate and seductive setting and suddenly Adrianna's only realities are the red-hot dust *and* Bryce....

Share the adventure—and the romance—
of A Year Down Under!

Available this month in
A YEAR DOWN UNDER

SECRET ADMIRER
by Susan Napier
Harlequin Presents #1554
Wherever Harlequin books are sold.

YDU-MY

Harlequin is proud to present our best authors and their best books. Always the best for your reading pleasure!

Throughout 1993, Harlequin will bring you exciting books by some of the top names in contemporary romance!

In June,
look for
*Threats and
Promises* by

BARBARA DELINSKY

The plan was to make her nervous....

Lauren Stevens was so preoccupied with her new looks and her new business that she really didn't notice a pattern to the peculiar "little incidents"—incidents that could eventually take her life. However, she did notice the sudden appearance of the attractive and interesting Matt Kruger who *claimed* to be a close friend of her dead brother....

Find out more in THREATS AND PROMISES . . . available wherever Harlequin books are sold.